# Alexis cupcake crush

This book is a work of fiction. Any references to historical events, real people, or real places are used fictitiously. Other names, characters, places, and events are products of the author's imagination, and any resemblance to actual events or places or persons, living or dead, is entirely coincidental.

SIMON SPOTLIGHT
An imprint of Simon & Schuster Children's Publishing Division
1230 Avenue of the Americas, New York, New York 10020
First Simon Spotlight hardcover edition May 2016

Text by Elizabeth Doyle Carey
Chapter header illustrations and design by Laura Roode
For information about special discounts for bulk purchases, please contact
Simon & Schuster Special Sales at 1-866-506-1949
or business@simonandschuster.com.
Manufactured in the United States of America 0416 FFG
2 4 6 8 10 9 7 5 3 1
ISBN 978-1-4814-6060-6 (pbk)
ISBN 978-1-4814-6061-3 (hc)
ISBN 978-1-4814-6062-0 (eBook)
Library of Congress Control Number 2016933194

CUPCAKE DIARIES

# Alexis cupcake crush

by coco simon

Simon Spotlight
New York London Toronto Sydney New Delhi

# CHAPTER 1

## Health Cakes

I took a big bite of a chocolate cupcake. "Mmm! Yummy! Vitamins and minerals!" I mumbled through the crumbs. But it was not yummy. Not yummy at *all*. "Ugh. These are horrible!" I yelled, and ran to the garbage to spit out my bite. "Sorry, Katie," I added sheepishly.

Emma and Mia laughed and Katie shook her head, but she was smiling.

The Cupcake Club was helping me out—*again!*—with a project, but for once it was something we were all experts in: cupcakes! This time, it was my project for the science fair, and I had decided to prove that cupcakes are good for you. I know, it sounds crazy—like yet another marketing scheme of mine—but it turns out it's true. Under certain circumstances, anyway.

So, according to my research, chocolate is good for you; especially dark chocolate. It is good for your blood and liver and cholesterol, and when you eat it, it releases endorphins, which relax you and make you feel happy. So, dark chocolate cupcakes with dark chocolate frosting are a must for the science fair. It's just a teeeeeny bit difficult to make dark chocolate taste really good without adding lots of sugar. (The bad thing about sugar is that it cancels out a lot of the healthy things about dark chocolate.) That's why improving sugarless taste is one thing we were working on in our "test kitchen," which was at Emma's house today.

Another way cupcakes can be good for you is if you swap out unhealthy ingredients for healthier ones. Like, instead of oil or butter, you can use applesauce, and instead of sugar, you can swap in either a sugar substitute, like stevia, or something naturally sweet, like sweet potatoes. Katie's really good at that kind of thing, because she just intuitively understands the principles of baking. My mom would be too, if she were a baker, 'cause she's really into healthy eating. But for her, healthy eating *excludes* cupcakes, and I think that is very, very sad. (And so does my dad, who *loves* cupcakes!)

If we can reduce the sugar and fat in our basic cupcake and frosting recipes, and up the dark chocolate, and then add fruit or veggies, then we can have a healthy recipe I can use for the science fair (not to mention samples I can hand out to the judges!). It's just been really slow going, and honestly, it's starting to seem like we'll never get them to taste good.

Mia's convinced if we make them look pretty enough, people will just eat them and not care, but I disagree, and so does Emma.

"It's not about looks!" said Emma.

"Easy for you to say," I teased. Emma's a model, and you know how really pretty people can sometimes take their looks for granted and, like, not notice them? She's like that. I suppose it's a good quality, but it can be kind of annoying, anyway.

Emma rolled her eyes. "You know what I mean."

Mia nodded. "I disagree. They have to be visually appealing."

"Mia's right," said Katie, her brow furrowed in concentration. "A lot of our perception is visual, even when it comes to taste. A good appearance makes us imagine one thing, while a bad appearance makes us imagine something else. Same with the aroma. If they smell good, that's half the battle.

You should make all that part of your research too."

I sat on a stool in Emma's kitchen. "Well, we definitely don't want people imagining . . ." I lifted a jar Katie had emptied into the new batter, and read the label. "Sweet potato puree? Yuck!"

"You'd be surprised," Katie said wisely.

I sighed. "That's why we pay you the big bucks, Katie. You're the taste doctor." I shrugged and pulled over the notebook I was using to keep track of the recipes to see what Katie had written in it. What I saw there was much more to my liking: quantities, measurements, pricing, calorie counts. . . . In a word, *numbers*! My favorite thing.

"Six ninety-nine for one little can of sweet potatoes?" I asked incredulously.

"They're organic, and they're pricey when they're processed like that. You could bake and scoop your own. It would be a lot cheaper, but they might not be as smooth as the professionally pureed ones," said Katie.

I pushed the jar away. "Well, let's just see how they taste. Maybe they're worth it, and we'll scrimp on something else."

The phone rang, and Emma went to answer it. She took a message and rejoined us.

"I've heard of people even using baby food," said Emma.

"Eww! In baked goods?" I asked.

"Uh-huh," Emma said, giggling. She picked up a yucky cupcake and tried to feed it to me, like I was a baby. "Open up, Lexi . . . ," she said in baby talk.

I clamped my mouth shut and shook my head.

"Come on! Yummy, yummy!" she joked, while wiggling the cupcake toward my mouth, like she was feeding a toddler.

I closed my eyes and shook my head harder, and she grabbed my chin to try to force open my mouth. I started laughing, and we were play-wrestling. I fell off the stool. Right then, Emma's brother Matt, the crush of my life, strolled in from practice.

He looked at me on the floor and then at Emma trying to shove the cupcake at me, and he shook his head, laughing. "If only people knew what went on behind the closed doors of the Cupcake Club. I could sell a magazine article about it for a fortune!"

"Please don't!" I cried, jumping to my feet.

"How much is my silence worth to you?" he joked.

I waved my arm at the dozen healthy (and awful) cupcakes on the counter. "These are all yours!" I said generously.

Matt's eyes lit up. "Seriously?"

I shared a smile with the other Cupcakers. "Uh-huh!"

Then he looked at me skeptically. "What's the catch?" He narrowed his eyes and lifted a cupcake to inspect it.

"Why would there be a catch?" I asked innocently.

Matt looked at the cupcake suspiciously. He turned it all around. It was small and dense, and the dark chocolate frosting was thick and glossy. It looked delicious. Next, Matt lifted it to his nose and gave it a whiff.

Katie nudged me. "See? Looks and smell count."

"Hmm. Good observation," I agreed.

We all stood with bated breath as Matt took a tentative nibble. He looked at us looking at him, and his brow furrowed. "It's . . ." He was about to say "good," but then the lack of sugar hit him.

He spun and hurried to the garbage and spat his cupcake on top of mine.

"*Blech!* Who forgot the sugar?!" he cried.

We all giggled.

"They're healthy cupcakes. They're good for you!" I chirped.

"Yeah, because you try one bite and then you

don't eat the rest. That's why it's good for you," Matt retorted, scowling. He wagged his finger at me as I laughed. "You owe me, missy!"

"They're my project for the science fair. You're our guinea pig," I admitted.

Matt got a funny look on his face. "The science fair? Already? Oh. That's cool. Who are you partners with?"

"Partners? Who gets partners for a science fair?" I laughed, still giddy. "I'm my own partner. Plus my silent partners, the Cupcake Club!"

Mia waved and I laughed again.

"Oh. Well, that should be a winner," said Matt, but he didn't sound superenthusiastic. He hoisted his backpack onto his shoulder and turned to go up to his room.

"Sam Perry called," Emma said as he retreated.

"Who?" Matt turned back around.

"Sam Perry?" said Emma.

"Who's Sam Perry?" I asked.

Emma shrugged.

Matt had a funny look on his face that I couldn't read. "New at school," he said, and he wandered off.

"Who's Sam Perry?" I repeated to Emma when Matt was out of earshot.

"I have no idea," she said, looking at her nails.

"Weird. Never heard of him," I said. I wondered briefly why Matt had acted so odd. But maybe I was just imagining things.

Emma glanced at me like she was going to say something, but then she seemed to change her mind and instead said, "Katie, what about applesauce?"

Katie nodded. "We can try that. It's always the first suggestion. It's just that applesauce does have a lot of sugar in it itself. You kind of might as well use real sugar."

Katie made a third batter now, opening the jar of applesauce and measuring out the proper amount. I like applesauce (much more than sweet potatoes), so I had high hopes for this batch.

Meanwhile, we needed to start brainstorming about our real work, the kind that earns money. My favorite kind!

I opened the ledger where we keep track of all our business and scanned the recent entries. "Oh, we've got a sweet sixteen coming up," I said. "In two weekends."

"Cool. That could be fun. Just for starters, I'm thinking all pink and ruffly, like a *quinceañera*," said Mia, referencing the Latina rite of passage she was looking forward to in her own life.

"Whose party is it?" asked Katie.

"Um, Martine Donay?" I wasn't sure I was pronouncing the name right. I'd never heard of her.

*"Martine Donay?!"* said Mia incredulously. "She's having a sweet sixteen? With *cupcakes*?"

Katie and I exchanged a worried glance. "Um, yeah?" I said.

Mia laughed and smacked the counter with her palm. "Wow. I've seen it all now. Who'd a-thunk it? Martine Donay!"

"Who *is* this person?" I asked. I was getting a little annoyed. "Emma, do you know her?"

Emma smiled. "Yup. She's not exactly the sweet sixteen–type. She lives around the corner. I see her sometimes, but I don't think she would know me."

"She's a friend of Dan's, for starters," said Mia, referring to her stepbrother, who's a heavy-metal music nut.

"Oh," I said. That told me a lot.

"A total rocker chick," continued Mia. "Black leather, ripped jeans, chains—the works. I can't imagine what kind of cupcakes she'd want."

"Well, it was her mother who contacted us," I said, looking at my notes.

"We'll need to get in touch with them and see what they're hoping for," said Emma. "This ought to be interesting."

I made a note in the ledger and agreed to contact Mrs. Donay and set up a meeting.

"Anything else lined up for that weekend?" asked Katie.

"Two kids' birthday parties—a seven-year-old boy, Sawyer Reese, and a five-year-old girl, Libby Murray—and this weekend, only Mona's minis, as usual, and book club for Mrs. Gormley. She requested the bacon caramel cupcakes. I think it's that same book club we've baked for in the past; it just moves around from house to house. They love our bacon cupcakes."

"Best idea I ever had!" crowed Emma as she helped Katie ladle the two revised batches of batter into the cupcake liners in the muffin pan. "And you all laughed at me!"

"Live and learn, that's one of my mottoes," I said with a shrug.

"Oh, Alexis, what *isn't* one of your mottoes?" teased Mia.

"It does help to have organizing principles, you know," I said with a sniff, but I was really only pretending to be annoyed. I know my friends love me and all my quirkiness. That's why the Cupcake Club is so much fun. I get to totally relax and be my true self with these three girls.

"Yes, you're very organized," agreed Katie with a gentle teasing smile. "So, what are we doing for the kids' birthdays?"

I looked back at my notes again. "Okay, they each only need two dozen. Sawyer is having a dinosaur-themed party with a dig for 'fossils,' so he wants something that looks like mud. Libby wants pink ballet-themed cupcakes with fluffy pink frosting."

"Cute!" said Mia. We all nodded.

"Any other Cupcake business?" asked Emma.

I glanced around the ledger page. "Well, we were talking about getting a quote from Matt for some new flyers to hand out to new clients."

"Ooh, good idea!" agreed Mia. "He does such a nice job," she said to Emma. "My mom recommended him to her boss for their next graphic design needs."

"Cool! Thanks! I'll tell him," said Emma.

Matt is very talented at graphic design and computer stuff. We've used him for posters and flyers and mailings and more, and we've always been really impressed by his talent. I especially like using him for projects 'cause then I get to hang out with him more and it gives me an excuse to text/e-mail/call him!

"I'll send him an e-mail for a quote." I made a note to myself. "We should brainstorm about what we're looking to say about ourselves and what we offer."

It's pretty cool how far we've come as a business from when we first started, and I'm not saying that to brag just 'cause I'm the CEO. I like thinking about things like mission statements and profit-and-loss sheets; these are the things I work on in the Future Business Leaders of America, a club at school, and they always come in handy in real life.

"Just do a quick thing at the top, like, 'Four stylish friends plus professional baking experience times good taste equals the Cupcake Club,'" suggested Mia.

"That is awesome!" I replied, writing as fast as I could to get it all down. I love math, so any math-themed thing is up my alley.

Katie looked thoughtful. "Or you could do a recipe, like 'two cups experience, one cup great taste, one cup style' . . . uh . . ."

Mia warmed to Katie's idea and kept it going. "'Four tablespoons friendship . . .'"

"'A splash of zest'!" added Emma.

"'Makes: one great party treat'!" I added.

"That's so good. I love it," Mia said, grinning.

"What about your equation idea, though? I loved that too," I said.

Mia shook her head. "No, save that for something else. I mean, write it in the ledger and we'll use it later."

"Okay. This is great. Thanks!"

"How much longer on these cupcakes?" asked Mia.

Katie looked at the timer. "Nine minutes."

"I hope these work!" I said nervously. "No offense," I added.

"None taken," said Katie. "I hope they work too. Anyway, it could be good for us to offer a healthy option in cupcakes too."

I smacked my head. "Of course! Maybe if we hit on the right thing, we can put that on our flyer too. Like, 'Now introducing our line of healthy options . . .'"

We cleaned up and chatted, and soon the cupcakes were out of the oven and frosted. Katie arranged them on two plates, and we all sampled one of each.

I tried the applesauce first, cautiously this time. The texture was good; they were nice and moist. I rolled the bite around in my mouth and found it pleasantly sweet—not overly so (like a regular cupcake) but pretty darn good!

"Hey! The applesauce ones are pretty good!" I said in surprise.

Mia was wide-eyed. She swallowed. "The sweet potato ones are *really* good!"

I made a face—ew, sweet potato puree—but I reached for one and then popped a bite into my mouth. She was right!

"Oh, Katie!" I said through my mouthful of cake. "*These* are delicious!"

Katie was chewing thoughtfully. "Thanks," she said. "I think the sweet potato ones are actually the better ones." She swallowed. "But do they have kind of a funny aftertaste?"

I moved my tongue around in my mouth. "I don't know. Maybe. Not bad, though."

"I think they're great," said Emma. "But do you want me to call in the experts?"

*Any chance to see Matt!* "Sure!" I agreed.

"They're not that picky, remember," warned Emma. "Hey, boys!" she yelled.

Soon, Emma's brothers—Jake, Matt, and Sam—were thundering into the kitchen, and the cupcakes were quickly depleted. They resoundingly voted for the sweet potato version, and Katie decided to reuse the applesauce concept as a new healthy apple-cinnamon recipe for the fall.

"Are these really good for me?" Jake asked, not believing us.

I nodded solemnly. "Packed with veggies. Can you tell?"

Jake shook his head. "You're tricking me!"

I looked at my friends. "That's just the reaction we were hoping for!" We all high-fived.

# CHAPTER 2

## Rock On!

Mrs. Donay suggested that the Cupcakers stop by after four o'clock on Monday to meet with her and Martine about the sweet sixteen cupcakes. At lunch in the cafeteria that day, we giggled in nervous anticipation about what she might ask for.

"What if she wants all-black cupcakes?" asked Emma.

"We've done that before, haven't we?" said Katie. "Can you look it up?" she asked me.

I nodded and made a note to myself. "I'm pretty sure. We've done a blackout cake. That's close."

"We could do dark chocolate healthy cupcakes!" Katie said brightly.

"I'm not sure health is Martine's first priority," said Mia. "She's so pale and thin."

"You can't judge a book by its cover," admonished Emma.

"Easy for you to say!" I joked.

"Why?" asked Emma suddenly all serious.

I always tease Emma about being a model. It's kind of fun, and she's an easy mark.

"Oh, just . . ." I could feel my cheeks growing red. One bad thing about being a redhead is you blush easily and often.

"You mean because I make money modeling, right?" pressed Emma.

"Em, she was just joking," cautioned Mia.

I raised my palms innocently. "I'm just teasing . . . ," I said. "No need to be so touchy."

Emma sighed. "I'm sorry I have a certain look that they seem to like out there in the world. I don't think it makes me better than anyone, and I don't think I'm conceited or anything like that, do you?"

"Wow. Sorry. I'm . . . I didn't know it bothered you so much."

Katie and Mia were looking on with worried expressions.

"Well, it does. So please stop," said Emma. "I'm not trying to be mean, but I really am sick of it, okay?"

"Totally, jeez. Sorry." I looked down at my lunch tray and fiddled with a straw wrapper.

"Okay, that was awkward," joked Mia.

Katie smiled, but Emma and I didn't.

"Come on, you two," said Katie.

I glanced up, and behind Emma's shoulder, across the cafeteria, I spotted Matt walking in, looking adorable in a blue chambray shirt and beat-up khakis. My sour mood brightened. There was construction in the high school cafeteria, so both of our grades had to share a cafeteria. I was sure he'd come over to say hi to us. I started fussing with my hair to make sure it was perfectly and naturally awesome looking.

But just then, a girl sitting at a table near the door jumped up and ran over to him, chatting excitedly and gesturing at her table. Matt looked a little caught off guard, but then he smiled and nodded and then went to get his lunch.

*Who on earth is that?* I wondered. And then, *Please don't let him sit with her; please don't let him sit with her,* I chanted in my mind. But not a moment later, he appeared, tray in hand, and went to join her table, where she began chattering excitedly at him again.

I didn't recognize the girl. She had long,

straw-colored straight hair, and she wasn't too tall or too short, and she was fit and sporty looking. She was sitting with girls in the grade above me, so she must've been older. She was very pretty; I had to admit it. Fresh-faced and cheerleaderish, but not tacky. I was dying to ask Emma who she was, but obviously I couldn't, since I now hated Emma and Matt and actually the whole darn Taylor family. (Kidding. Sort of.)

"Well, I guess I'll be going now," I said.

"I'm not in a fight with you, Lexi-lou," Emma said nicely, using our most secret preschool nickname.

I grimaced at the name. "I'm not in a fight with you either," I said.

"Let's all meet outside school at three thirty, go get a snack, and walk to the Donays' together, okay?" said Mia brightly.

"And no more fighting," added Katie, wagging her finger at us, mock-seriously.

"Fine," I said grouchily.

"Who's fighting?" kidded Emma.

"Hmph," I said. I stalked out of the cafeteria without so much as glancing at Matt again.

The bad vibes from lunch were honestly forgotten or blown away by the time we met up outside school later, though I reminded myself not to tease Emma about being pretty anymore. Those days were over for sure. But it was a gorgeous afternoon, sunny and warm with blue skies, and we were all jazzed by our freedom and in good moods. I had put the Matt lunch scenario out of my mind and resolved to not worry about it—it was just a one-off.

We played "step on a crack, you'll break your best friend's back" all the way to the Donays' house and were laughing and pushing and shoving one another the whole time. When we reached Emma's block, we passed the Donay house without realizing it and had to double back to find it; it wasn't what we were expecting for such a rocker chick.

The house was adorable—a small white Cape Cod with a little wing off each side and really pretty landscaping, with lots of blue and white flowers blooming.

"It's so pretty!" Katie exclaimed breathlessly.

We climbed a few brick stairs and ventured up the walk to the front door, and then I rang the doorbell and stepped back. Because the house was elevated, the view from the front door was really pretty—all treetops from the neighboring houses, and the air was filled with birdsong.

"Not exactly what you would picture . . . ," began Mia, and then the door opened.

"Hello! You must be the Cupcake Club!" said a woman with a friendly voice and a strong accent.

I turned to find a very pleasant, pretty woman at the door, grinning widely at us. She was petite and a little curvy, with red hair just like mine, and fair skin and dimples. Along with a warm smile, she was wearing a chic white silk blouse with a floppy bow at the neck and high-waisted black trousers with black high heels.

"Hi, Mrs. Donay, I'm Alexis," I said, sticking out my hand.

"Lovely to meet you," she said. I loved her accent but felt like it would be rude to ask where she was from.

"And you, too. Let me introduce the rest of the team," I began, introducing all around.

"Please do come in. Martine is just inside in the kitchen. Martine, *alors*! *Elles sont ici!*"

"Oh, are you French?" I asked, recognizing the language.

"Well, French Canadian, actually. But raised in Quebec, speaking French. Everyone speaks it there," said Mrs. Donay.

"Cool," I marveled. "I would love to live in

another country for a while when I grow up."

We passed through the front hall, the dining room, and into the kitchen, chatting as we walked. I tried to look at everything in the pretty house, but it was hard to take in. My main impression was: elegant.

The kitchen had a marble-topped table on an iron base, with little bistro chairs around it, and a neatly patterned black-and-white–tiled floor. The lights were hanging lanterns, and the whole thing looked really French, actually. In the middle of all this was Martine, exactly as Mia had described her: jet-black hair in a choppy cut; pale white skin; heavy black eye makeup; a serious expression on her face; and lots of black denim, piercings, and chains. She was tiny—short and waifish—with a heart-shaped face and a pointed, pixieish little chin. She looked like Tinker Bell, if Tink ever turned Goth.

I was totally intimidated and hoped my surprise at her appearance didn't show on my face when I greeted her. I expected her to be as sour as her mom was sweet.

"Hi, Martine, I'm Alexis," I said in a professional manner, putting out my hand. But then Martine smiled, and her serious face was transformed. She had her mother's dimples and a similar wide grin, with pretty blue eyes that turned up at the corners when she smiled.

"Hi," Martine said shyly, shaking my hand. In surprise, I introduced everyone, and Martine continued to smile.

"*Alors*, let's all sit at the table and have *quelque chose à manger*—something to eat!" said Mrs. Donay. She went and lifted a heavy tray from the counter and brought it to the table.

There were two bottles of sparkling lemonade in tall frosty glass bottles, stacked bistro glasses, a plate piled high with fancy lacy cookies, and nice periwinkle-blue linen napkins. Mrs. Donay doled out drinks and snacks as we chatted about the weather, and when I took a bite of the cookie, I nearly swooned.

"Oh, Mrs. Donay! Did you make these? They're incredible!"

"Ah, *mais non*. I wish! I picked them up on my way home from work. They are from the French bakery two towns over in the new shopping center." She giggled a tinkling girlish laugh. "I can't cook my way out of—how do you say?—a paper sack!"

Martine laughed at her kindly. "'Bag,' Maman,

not 'sack'! And maybe you can't cook, but you are the best at presentation!"

Her mother pursed her lips modestly and nodded in agreement. "I can put take-out on pretty plates and make it look enchanting. That's half the war!"

"'Battle,' Maman," said Martine. "Half the battle." She rolled her eyes, but it was only in jest; it was more for her mother's benefit.

They were really cute together, the mother and daughter. I was so used to slightly torturing my parents and watching my friends annoy theirs that it was refreshing to see a mother and daughter be nice to each other. They were almost like friends.

I smiled. "So, Martine, what are you thinking for your birthday cupcakes?"

Martine grinned mischievously. "Well, let me start by saying, I really love your work. I've had cupcakes that Dan—I think he is someone's brother?"

Mia raised her hand. "Step," she acknowledged. "But we live together."

Martine nodded. "He's brought some of your cupcakes to gigs and rehearsals—we jam in a band together sometimes—and they are just soooo delicious! I'm not really the cupcake type. Or the 'sweet sixteen'–type, either," she said, making quotation marks in the air by her head. "But when my mother talked me into having a party, I knew I had to have your cupcakes for dessert."

"Wow! We're flattered!" I said.

"Do you remember what flavors you had? Or do you have an idea of something you might like or want in terms of flavor?" asked Katie.

I had opened my notebook to take notes, and my pen was poised.

Martine pushed her hair back behind her ear, which made her look like a little kid. She squinted her eyes to remember. "I like the cake that was chocolate, I think? And frosting—vanilla. Black and white. Pretty boring."

"Not boring," said Katie. "A delicious and simple canvas for an elegant design."

Mia leaned in. "What are you thinking for the party theme? We can tie the cupcake design into that."

Mrs. Donay exclaimed rapidly, *"Ooh la, la, la, la, la, la!"* and flapped her hands—in excitement or nervousness, it was hard to tell which.

"The party is themed to be like CBGB, which was a famous rock club in New York City that closed down." Martine grinned. "It's going to be in a warehouse, with really loud heavy-metal music, big candles everywhere, and a studio booth so people can cut their own tracks using a synthesizer."

"Wow!" said Emma. "That sounds amazing!" Emma has an on-again, off-again flirtation with heavy metal that the rest of us don't share. (That's the polite way of putting it.)

"Do you think? I hope so! The attire is 'Rockin' Out in Black.' My mother will get piles of accessories . . . fake chains and nose rings and things for people to wear to dress up if they want, and on the same table, we're having colored hairspray and mini black lipsticks and stuff, for people to really go wild."

"Awesome!" It actually did sound fun, though if I were going, I'd wear earplugs.

"I can't wait! So anyway, maybe the cupcakes could have something to do with all this, please?" Martine asked politely.

I looked at her mother, who was nodding. It was so funny because Mrs. Donay was so conservative and normal looking, and Martine's appearance was so out there. I would have assumed there'd be a lot of crankiness or frustration between the two of them, but there just wasn't. Maybe Martine's mom liked how her daughter looked, or maybe she thought it was a phase she'd outgrow. Either way, it was remarkable. And a relief.

I could see Mia's creative wheels spinning as we tied up the loose ends about quantity and date. We adjourned by saying we'd make a few sample designs for them to see this weekend. The party was two weeks off, so we'd have some time to get it right. Right?

Outside the house after our meeting, the four of us were speechless. We walked down the brick steps and onto the sidewalk, and then everyone began to speak at once.

"That was so . . . ," began Katie.

"Okay, that was totally *not* what I was expecting . . . ," said Mia.

Emma's mouth just hung open.

"Guys! Wait till we at least get around the corner before we start discussing this. Discretion is the backbone of our business! Shh!" I cautioned in a low voice.

We walked the rest of the block in silence, and then we burst out chattering again.

"Wow! She was so nice!" said Emma.

"I know!" I agreed. "I thought she'd be . . ."

"Mean or something, because of how she dresses and whatever . . . ," supplied Katie.

"And she and her mom got along so well . . . ," said Mia.

"That was really fun!" I summed up. "I guess like Emma said, you really can't judge a book by its cover!"

Katie agreed. "There's always more than meets the eye. That's one of my mottoes," she added with a giggle, elbowing me so I'd know she was teasing.

"Ha-ha," I said.

"What in the world are we going to make?" Mia moaned.

I patted her on the arm. "Don't worry. You'll think of something. That's why we pay you the big bucks."

"Oh, *that's* why!" said Mia, laughing.

"I guess we have to use our usual brainstorm session technique," said Emma. "Time to start searching the Internet for ideas!"

# CHAPTER 3

## Research

"Lex, by the way, what's first prize for the science fair?" whispered Emma.

"You mean besides the glory of winning, would there be, like, a trophy or something?" I whispered back.

"Or maybe some cold, hard cash?" Mia wiggled her eyebrows.

"I have to check," I said. "I'm going to look at the contest rules on the website tonight when I start to organize my presentation."

We were doing our homework after school in the library because I needed to look up calorie and health information for my science project. Well, actually, I needed Katie to help me do it, because she was the food person and knew what to look for.

Emma and Mia came along to keep us company.

Katie's forehead rested in her hand. She was poring over charts in some giant, thick health books.

"Thank you so much, Katie," I murmured. "Is it really hard?"

Katie looked up at me and nodded. "It's just . . . It all depends on what you think is the most important for the 'healthy' aspect. Low in sugar? Fewer calories? High in vitamins and minerals? Low in fat? Do you have your thesis?"

"Hmm." I tapped my lip with my pen as I thought. I guess I did need to clarify my thesis for the project. Should it be "Cupcakes Don't Have to Be Bad for You"? But I don't want to imply that cupcakes *are* bad for you because, obviously, that could take a big bite out of our business! So I decided it would be "Cupcakes Are Good for You! (But Only Certain Ones)." I sighed.

"What's the matter, Lex?" Emma asked kindly.

I explained my dilemma, and the other girls thought about it too. I love my friends, I must say. They are so helpful!

"What about, 'Cupcakes Aren't the Worst Thing in the World for You!'?" joked Mia.

"Ha-ha," I said.

Emma was thinking for real, though. Finally, she

said, "What about something like, 'Cupcakes Can Be Good for You!'?"

"Hmmm . . . ," I said, pondering it. "I think that works! Right?" I looked at Katie, who had the best grasp of the situation, and she was nodding.

"Yes. I think that's safe and accurate," she agreed.

"And most important, provable!"

"Will you need to give the info on an 'unhealthy' cupcake for contrast?" asked Mia.

"Oh. Hmm. Yes. I guess so," I said. "I hate to criticize our own good work, though. . . ."

We were quiet for a moment, and then Emma had another brilliant suggestion. "Hey! Just use a boxed cupcake mix and canned frosting for contrast! No need to use our own cupcakes, right?"

"Eureka!" I cried, slamming my palm onto the tabletop.

"Shhhh!" shushed the librarian.

I blushed, and the girls and I all exchanged guilty looks. "Oops. But that is genius, Em. Thanks!" I was so happy! The Cupcake Club had solved all my problems, yet again. As I sat basking in my happiness, the door to the library opened, and in walked Matt.

"Matt!" I called in a joyful whisper. I wanted to share the good news, but really, I just wanted to connect with him and flirt a little since I was in such a great mood. What could be better than the arrival of a great idea and your crush, all in one minute?!

But he didn't hear me because he was talking to the girl who came in right behind him. The same girl from the cafeteria the other day. They were speaking in whispers because we were in the library, so their heads were kind of close together, and then she said something that made him laugh. Watching them, I felt like I was going to be sick. Now, I was mortified I had called out to him, and I prayed he wouldn't notice us over here. I sank down in my chair, my face flushing beet red. I couldn't meet my friends' eyes, but I was sure they were looking back and forth between Matt and me.

After a few painful seconds, which felt like an hour, Emma said softly, "They're gone. They didn't see us."

When I didn't reply, she said, "Lexi?"

I looked over at her. I know my misery was written all over my face. "Is that his girlfriend?" I asked, in pain.

Emma tilted her head to the side thoughtfully. "No. I don't think so. No."

"Wait, so, 'no,' or 'I don't think so'?" I asked.

"Well, I haven't heard one way or the other," said Emma, looking away. "Probably not, though. I would have heard something, I'm sure."

"Not if he's anything like Dan," said Mia. "Sorry," she apologized to me. "But teenage boys don't tell anyone anything about their personal lives."

"Who is that girl?" I asked Emma, cringing.

"Um, I think she's Samantha Perry."

That name sounded familiar. *Why?* I racked my brain. "Wait! *Sam* Perry? Like who called when we were at your house the other day?"

Emma shrugged. "I guess?"

Now I was annoyed. "Do so many girls call Matt that it's hard to keep track?" I sputtered.

"Hey, I'm just his sister! I'd be the last one to know anything about his personal life, so don't get mad at me!" she said indignantly.

"Okay. You're right. I'm sorry." I backed down. There was no point in getting mad at Emma. None of this was her fault.

My heart rate was slowing down, and I could feel that my flush had subsided. "You know, whatever. It's not like we're together, anyway!" I said huffily. Was I just trying to convince myself? Sure. But what were my other options? To cry? To mourn a relationship that never officially was?

My friends looked at me and then at one another. No one said anything. It was a tense moment.

"It's fine. Anyway. Okay. So, what else?"

Mia shrugged slightly at Katie and Emma, and so they all carried on.

Katie said, "I think your best bet here is to go for high vitamin content, low in fat, low in sugar, high in fiber. If we do the dark chocolate, you can say 'Packed with antioxidants,' too."

I took a deep breath. "Okay. That all sounds good." I began making notes, despite hearing people moving in the library behind me. I willed myself not to turn around to see if it was Matt and Samantha. I just needed to stay focused.

"So what are we saying for quantities?" I asked Katie.

"Hey," Mia said to Emma. "Want to take a homework break and search rock-and-roll cupcake images while these guys finish this?"

Emma nodded. "Sure. Great. Let's go."

They left the table and went to a bank of computers in the corner of the room. Katie and I continued on, laboriously copying the recipe and health information and liberally using my trusty calculator. (Phones, and therefore calculator apps, were not allowed in the library. Luckily, I never leave home without my calculator!) Every once in a while I'd look up at the sound of people entering or exiting the library, but it was never Samantha and Matt. On the one hand, this was good, because I really wanted to finish our work and get out of there before we saw them. On the other, it bothered me they had so much to do together in the library!

Suddenly, Emma appeared at our table. "You've got to come see these awesome cupcakes! They look hard to make, though, and Mia's not sure we can pull it off."

Katie and I stood and crossed the room to see what Mia had up on the screen. Emma was right. The cupcakes *were* awesome! There were a bunch of different concepts, but most involved pretty elaborate fondant toppers, like musical notes, mini electric guitars, and little heart-shaped vinyl records that looked like tattoos with the words LOVE TO ROCK on a banner across them.

"Aren't they great?" asked Mia with a smile.

"Totally," I agreed. Despite my bad mood about Matt, I can never stay completely unhappy when I am in the presence of cupcake greatness. "But they would be a lot of work. And probably a little pricier than what we normally do."

Mia nodded. "I know. But the Donays are so nice. And I feel like we could tap into a great new high school market with these."

I swatted Mia playfully on the arm. "You're just trying to butter me up by talking about marketing, aren't you?"

Mia grinned wickedly. "Busted! But can't we try these, Alexis? Please? Martine will love them!"

I sighed. "Why don't we meet tomorrow at Katie's, where all the good decorating stuff is, and we'll see how quickly and easily we can make these things, okay?"

Emma suddenly turned to the computer she was at. "Guys! Look! Um, come see this thing!" She was typing frantically, and we all scooted over to her side.

"What?"

"What is it?" I asked.

We leaned in as images started to appear on the screen. There were photos of weird people from really long ago (like the 1970s) dressed all crazy, like rockers, and a small dark nightclub.

"What is this?" I asked, peering more closely.

"Uh, this is CBGB, that club that Martine mentioned," said Emma, looking nervously over our backs toward the librarian on duty at the door.

"What's the matter? Do you think these are inappropriate?" I asked. "Too grungy for you?"

Emma swiveled her head back to the screen. "Um, what? No. They're fine. It's just shots of the outside and then the inside of the club, all empty. Ha! Anyway, I just . . . uh . . . wanted you all to see the reference. It's pretty gritty, right?"

We all nodded. "Gross," I agreed. Then we started back to our table.

"Wait!" said Emma, dragging us all back to the computer station. "Um . . . what about . . . if we search 'CBGB' and 'cupcakes'?"

"Um, okay?" said Katie. She crossed her arms, and we all stood, waiting.

Emma sat down again, started typing, looked back at the door, and then stood up. "Okay, never mind. Nothing good. I think we have everything we need, right?" She started back to our table again, and we followed her.

"Em, why are you acting so weird?" I asked.

"And jumpy?' said Mia.

Emma raised her eyebrows meaningfully at Mia, and I intercepted the look.

"What?" I asked.

Emma sighed. "It was just . . . Matt and Samantha were leaving a few minutes ago. I didn't want us to have to talk to them. Sorry." She shrugged.

We all stood there silent for a minute. Then I circled the table and put my arm across Emma's shoulder. "Thanks, Em," I said. "That would have stank."

She nodded.

"Okay, then," Mia said fake-cheerfully. "Should we go home?"

"Let's give it a minute, I think," Emma said quietly.

We packed up our things in silence. I felt sick with dread at the idea of running into Matt and Samantha. "I might just stay here for a bit," I said.

"Don't be ridiculous," said Mia. "You're coming with us!" She looped her arm through mine, swung her bag over her other shoulder, and strode out the door, giving a cheerful wave to the librarian, dragging me as she went. "Chin up, kid!" she whispered. "And smile!"

I followed her directions, even if my smile was forced, and I didn't look left or right as we headed for the nearest exit. We burst out of the library into the bright afternoon sunlight, and Mia asked, "A slice?"

I nodded, and she began to propel us straight to the nearby pizza parlor.

Katie and Emma followed along behind us. Suddenly, Mia stopped walking and looked me straight in the eye. "Alexis, listen to me. I've seen a lot of movies, and my mom was single for a while, so I know the drill. Never let a guy see you jealous."

I nodded again. "Okay."

"You don't want him to think you like him more than he likes you, that's another thing," Katie added.

Mia nodded knowledgeably. "And if you see him, don't even mention that other girl's name because, you'd be surprised. Guys can be kind of dense. Sometimes they don't even think of another girl that way until you mention it yourself, you know? So, don't."

"Huh" was all I could come up with.

Mia tried to think of more advice, but then she just shrugged. "Just . . . just don't worry, Alexis. There's usually more than meets the eye, you know?" "Mm-hmm," I agreed.

Katie piped up from behind us, "Yeah, so don't judge a book by its cover."

"I think that's becoming my new motto . . . ," I said with a moan.

# CHAPTER 4

## Tattoo Taboo

I had to search "Samantha Perry" when I got home. Here's what I learned about her: not much.

She has a private Facebook page, a private Instagram account (I even considered sending her a friend request but thought better of it), and her name is listed on the town newspaper site because they once asked her what her favorite thing about autumn was in an interview with, like, five other people. That's all. Now, I, on the other hand, appear on the Future Business Leaders of America home-page (as vice president); on our Cupcake Club website numerous times; on the ASPCA website as a volunteer and fund-raiser; and other miscella-neous local, charitable, and school events. Granted, my parents won't let me have a Facebook account, and my Instagram is private too, but I think I cast a pretty good shadow online. If you searched for me, you will learn that I am motivated, charitable, and busy, plus, you can see what I look like (which is sometimes good, sometimes bad, depending on the photo). With Samantha Perry . . . nothing!

I knew she was new and that I'd never seen (or maybe never noticed?) her before. I knew she was in the grade above me. Oh, and that she's been to the beach at least once, because her profile image on Instagram is a photo of a lifeguard's chair. In theory, it was for the best that there wasn't much online for me to obsess over. On the other hand, all it really meant was that I'd have to do some more digging. I just wasn't satisfied. And if I was going to have to battle an enemy, I needed to be armed with information!

The next day at school I kept my eyes wide open. Her thick blond hair was eye-catching, and twice I thought I'd spied her walking in the halls, but both times it turned out to be Tina Marshall from the seventh grade, who has similar hair.

*Finally,* I saw her a few people ahead of me on the lunch line. My stomach lurched when I spotted her. I almost felt like I was scared of her. Well,

I guess I was! I was afraid she was busy stealing the love of my life, that's what!

I studied her outfit carefully—plain white crew neck, with a plain powder-blue cotton pullover sweater on top and generic jeans. A pair of low-top, faded, green Chuck Taylors. She was dressed pretty simply. Okay, so not a fashionista like Mia. When she turned to talk to the girl next to her, I could see she wore just tiny gold earrings and no other jewelry. No makeup. So, kind of low-maintenance. Almost tomboyish. Hmm. Not good. If she'd been wearing piles of makeup, and jangly jewelry, and some way-too-old-for-her outfit, I would have breathed a sigh of relief. That would not be Matt Taylor's type. But Samantha Perry's outfit *was* Matt Taylor's type. In fact, she was dressed kind of like . . . me.

I watched her interact with the people around her. She seemed to be friends with the girl she was standing next to, Mackenzie Kurtz. Mackenzie was really nice and mellow. Just a cool girl without any attitude or a mean edge; friends with everyone in her grade, pretty much. If Samantha was friends with Mackenzie, well, that wasn't good either. It meant she was nice and not flashy or pushy. Also bad news for me.

Now, I needed to know the most important

piece of information. Was she sporty? I am athletic (I'm on the volleyball team) though not *super*sporty, like a jock working out all the time. But Matt really likes athletic people. After all, he spends most of his time doing sports. I remember once when these girls from our grade came by Emma's and tried to shoot baskets with Matt in the driveway. They were totally girly and silly and flirty and terrible at basketball, and Matt was totally turned off. Note to self: Check to see if Samantha Perry is good at sports and if so, which ones!

After I got my lunch, I joined Mia and Katie at their table. Emma hadn't arrived yet. I was miserable. I placed my tray with its plate of pasta with red sauce and small house salad on the table, and then I proceeded to not eat any of it. I was too heartsick.

Mia looked at me consolingly. "Lex, please don't be so upset!"

I sighed heavily. "I'm trying."

Katie tried to cheer me up with business news. "My mom's hygienist is hosting a baby shower next weekend and needs six dozen cupcakes, Lexi!"

"Mm-hmm," I said, nodding. I was craning my neck to see if I could see where Samantha Perry had sat and with whom.

"Are we up for that?" asked Katie.

"Yes, okay," I said distractedly.

"Even with the two birthday parties and the Donay event?" asked Mia.

"What?" I quickly snapped to attention, and they laughed.

"Do you think we can really do four events next weekend, plus Mona's standing order for the bridal salon?" asked Mia.

"No way! Seriously?" Now I was paying attention.

I looked at Mia and Katie. "I'm sorry. What are you asking me?"

Katie explained, and I slumped in my chair. "You know I'm always hungry for business . . . ," I began. "I hate to turn away clients. . . ."

"It *is* a lot, though," Mia said nervously.

I tapped my chin with my finger while I thought. "We could do some baking Thursday, some Friday, some Saturday?"

"It's the Donay decorating I'm worried about," said Katie.

We were silent for a second, and then Emma joined us. "Hey! Why so gloomy, everyone?" she asked cheerfully, setting down her tray.

Katie explained again, and Emma made a face as she swallowed her milk.

"Wow!" Emma exclaimed. "That's a lot of cupcakes. Even for us, at our best."

I had to admit, though—I kind of liked the idea of being distracted from the whole Matt and Samantha Perry thing. And what if we could do the baking at Emma's?! That would be three full days at her house. Surely Matt would come through at some point, and I could talk to him a little bit, plus bribe him with tons of free cupcakes.

I smacked my palm on the table, and everyone jumped. "I say let's do it!" I cried.

"Really?" asked Katie, surprised.

I shrugged. "Sure. Why not? I think we can handle it. And think how much money we'll make! And all that new exposure to teenagers and the hygienist's guests. We'll need to get flyers from Matt made before then, and maybe we could stick a small pile in with each delivery!"

The Cupcakers nodded and smiled. I could tell they were getting inspired.

"So we just need to be really organized. We can start doing the fondant stuff Tuesday at Katie's. We'll also do it on Wednesday. Then Thursday, Friday, Saturday, we can bake at Emma's . . . 'cause once we're set up there, it is just easier to stay in the same place. And then we'll assemble and deliver. . . ." I glossed over the baking details and headed right for delivery.

But Emma held up her hand and stopped me. "I'm sure it will be fine, but I just need to check with my family that we can do that for three days there. My mom totally doesn't mind, but sometimes other people have other stuff going on, and I don't want to mess anyone up. Okay?"

"Sure, sure," I agreed, and nodded, like it didn't matter at all to me where we baked. "Fine. Just . . . let's try to find out today. Tonight, I mean. If possible, please?" I smiled casually.

Emma gave me a strange look and said, "Right. Sure. Fine."

"Okay, and meanwhile, we need to do our samples this weekend for the Donays, okay? We can do it at my place?" I offered.

"I have to go my dad's this weekend, so let's do it at my house tomorrow!" said Mia. "We haven't done it there in a while."

"Great," I said, grinning widely. "Just great."

At Mia's on Thursday after school, we rolled out a huge amount of fondant. Katie had brought her edible paints and dyes, and she and Mia were working their artistic magic as Emma and I kind of supervised. We were baking dark chocolate cupcakes and white cupcakes and mixing up a batch of our darkest frosting and a simple batch of white buttercream. We'd flip the flavors for the black-and-white combos Martine was looking for.

Mia had printed out templates for electric guitars, drums, and a tattoo that looked like a scroll. (Her idea was to have the scroll say "Martine" in script.) Emma was trying to do some music notes freehand, using a printout for reference, but it was slow, precise work. She kept having to scrap them and start over.

Mia's stepbrother, Dan, came in about halfway through and checked out our handiwork.

"These are killer!" he said about the tattoo toppers.

Mia giggled. "You think?"

"They're sick," he said. "Sick" is Dan's highest compliment.

"I'll tell you, they're easier than the electric guitars . . . ," admitted Mia.

"And the music notes," added Emma with a sigh.

"I think they're really cool!" agreed Katie.

"Martine will love 'em," Dan said enthusiastically.

Mia looked at the rest of us. "Should we just call

it a go, then, on the scroll tattoos?" she asked.

I nodded. "Totally. They're edgy and stylish but kind of easy to make, right? And not too pricey."

"I could paint a little red rose on the edge of each one if you leave a little space too," suggested Katie. "That would look good, right?"

Mia squealed. "That would look awesome! Thanks! Let's try one."

We were all pretty happy about our plan and sure Martine and her mom would like it. Emma and I finished the cupcakes and frosting, and then Katie and Mia decorated the cakes. We put three of each kind in a cardboard bakery box, tied with a bow, and Emma dropped it off at the Donays' house on her way home.

When I got home I got right into my homework because I had a history test coming up, and I knew I'd have to work a little each day to get my study guide done, what with all the baking we had coming up. Then I spent some time on my recipes for the science fair and my research. I was going to make really good flyers to hand out, with professional calorie counts, like the ones on the backs of food packages and in recipes and stuff. It would look really great. I was also going to get paper party tablecloths with matching plates and napkins for my table, and some balloons, to make it look more like a party. That had been my mom's idea, and I really liked it. I was sure it would attract attention to my table, because if you just saw tons of boring booths, who wouldn't want to visit a table with brightly colored balloons you could see from clear across the gymnasium?!

I had a quick family dinner, and by the time I showered and got back to my desk it was nine o'clock. Mia and Katie had both texted to see if I'd heard from the Donays and what they thought of the cupcakes. So I quickly checked my e-mail and was stunned to find this:

> Dear Alexis,
>
> Many thanks for the cupcakes. They are delicious but the design on top will not do. *Je suis désolée.* Can you go please back to the drawing sheet?
>
> Mdm. Donay

Huh!

I sat staring at my screen in disbelief when another e-mail popped into my in-box. It was from Martine Donay:

Hi, Alexis,

I love the cupcakes! They are so cool and yummy! My mom hates tattoos, and we fight about me getting one all the time so she doesn't like the design, but I love it. I am working on her. Don't listen if she e-mails to say they won't work, okay?

Rock on!

Martine

Oh boy. What now? The Cupcake Club was stuck in the middle of a family dispute. It was kind of crazy, actually, that Mrs. Donay would go for all that wild stuff for the party and then draw the line at cupcake tattoos! But what could I say? The customer is always right. (That's one of *my* mottoes!) We needed a backup plan, and quick. I started searching and came up with a few ideas (edible sequins, anyone?), but none as great as what Mia had made. Finally, in exhaustion, I closed my computer and went to brush my teeth. Tomorrow at school I'd let the other Cupcakers know about what the Donays said. I couldn't face any more Cupcake business today.

# CHAPTER 5

## Ice Cream

I broke the news to the others at our lockers the next morning. I had had a poor night's sleep and awoke early, worrying about our situation. Should we go back to the drawing "sheet" ("board," I could just hear Martine correcting her mom) and come up with another plan, or wait and see?

Mia sighed. "We need a backup. Come on over again after school, and we'll rethink it."

"But I love the tattoos!" I cried.

"Maybe we could do an assortment," suggested Katie.

Emma grimaced. "I'll work harder on the music notes this time. By the way, other tricky news. Matt has a project at our house next Saturday for the science fair, so we can only do Thursday and Friday at my house. I'm sorry."

"Oh, I didn't know he was doing something for the fair," I said. "I mean, not that I would. Not that we check in or anything," I added awkwardly, looking down at my nails as if they were fascinating.

I looked up in time to see Emma shrug. "I didn't know either. Anyway, he said he needs the kitchen since he is hosting, so what could I say?"

"We can pick up the stuff Saturday morning from your house and move it over to mine," I offered.

"Thanks," Emma said with a grateful smile.

That afternoon, after much laborious stencil work, Katie and Mia prepared some awesome black fondant electric guitars and drums to send over to the Donays'. We didn't place them on cupcakes but rather laid them on a sheet of parchment in the bakery box, and Emma dropped them off on her way home. I also e-mailed Martine the link for the edible sequins and said we could go pick some up at the mall if she liked them.

We heard back quickly. Both Martine and Mrs. Donay loved the black fondant instruments, and, in addition, Martine said she loved the sequins.

Never mind the tattoos, and maybe we could do half instruments and half sequins?

Despite the fact that this required a trip to the mall, it would save us time in the long run, since sprinkling sequins on top of cupcakes would be much faster than cutting out fondant electric guitars! I e-mailed my parents to see if one of them would take us to the mall on Friday night from Emma's when they got home from work.

Then I forwarded the e-mails to the club and also added a note to Emma to see if she would mind asking Matt if he'd do some flyers for us for the weekend. She said she'd check and get back to me as soon as possible.

That night I slept like a baby. A very efficient, businesslike baby.

First of all, it is a good thing that the Taylors have a massive fridge in their garage. This meant we were able to prepare all our cupcake batter and frosting on Thursday night at Emma's and then stash it in the fridge to bake on Friday. On our docket we had the dirt cupcakes for Sawyer's birthday, the ballet cupcakes for Libby's birthday, Mona's white minis for the bridal salon, the hygienist's six dozen cupcakes, and then Martine Donay's sweet sixteen.

Even I had to admit it was our craziest weekend ever. I bet another science fair project could come out of this—perhaps something on efficiency and assembly lines?

On Friday we baked. And baked. And baked some more. Frankly, it was pretty boring. Luckily, the Taylors also have two ovens, so we could keep things turning. Meanwhile, Katie and Mia worked hard finishing up the fondant, and Emma and I stood around uselessly between batches until Matt showed up. (Of course, I did spend more than a few minutes primping in their powder room, and don't think I hadn't worn one of my favorite outfits: a cute skirt with leggings and a fitted top. Sporty but pretty.) Matt had agreed to do a flyer for us, but a quick and simple one, since he had to get ready for his science fair meeting the next day and couldn't spend a lot of time designing it for us.

"Hey, Cupcakers," he said shyly as he walked in.

The sound of his gravelly voice gave my stomach a lurch. I ducked into the pantry to compose myself. My heart was racing madly, and my face was immediately bright red.

"Matty boy!" called Mia. She is very relaxed around boys. More than I am. Maybe because she sort of has a brother now. I tried to channel her breezy confidence as I stood among the oversize boxes of cereal in the dark.

"Hi," Matt was saying. "So, I have a few minutes to do that flyer now, if you want?"

"No time like the present," I said, coming out of the pantry. On the outside I was cheerful but inside, I was suffering. I wanted desperately to ask him why he liked Samantha and if I stood a shot at all of ever being his girlfriend and why he liked her better than me, and on and on.

But I didn't.

I stood there grinning because I was just so happy to see him, and I didn't know what else to do or say. *And* it was the first time in a while that I'd seen him without Samantha, so that made me truly happy.

He grinned back at me. "So?" he asked.

"Right. Okay. So here's what we were thinking . . ." I opened up my laptop and nervously clicked on the file with our marketing ideas. Then Emma and I explained what we were looking for in terms of design and color. Matt nodded as we spoke, jotting down notes in the little notebook he keeps in his pocket. I don't think he noticed how nervous I was, thank goodness.

After we finished I stood there smiling at him

like an idiot. He smiled back. Then he said, "Got any extra cupcakes?"

And of course I always do for him, so I scrambled to get him a little plate, and I slathered some frosting on three cupcakes for him.

*"Voilá!"* I said, presenting him with the plate.

"Oh, international cupcakes?" he teased.

"No! But *that* is a great idea. I guess I just have French on the brain because of the Donays."

We chatted for a minute about all our weekend jobs, and then he said, "I'd better go get started on your flyer. I have to go to the mall for fair supplies in a bit, so I don't have a ton of time." He gathered up his things and began to leave.

"Oh, we have to go too!" I cried happily. "Want to come with us?" I blurted.

Matt was headed out of the kitchen. "Oh, thanks, that's nice, but I have a ride. They're picking me up."

"Okay, see you there!" I called. (Maybe too eagerly? Maybe I shouldn't have offered the ride? Ugh! Who *knew* what to do when it came to boys?!)

There was silence in the kitchen after Matt left, and I could hear him rummaging around upstairs in his room and settling down at his desk.

"He hates me," I whispered.

"Are you insane?" said Mia with a laugh. "He's totally into you!"

"Yeah, Alexis. Even if it's just as a friend, he *really* likes you," agreed Katie.

"What do you mean 'just as a friend'?" I asked, wheeling around in a panic.

Katie looked nervous. "No. I mean, I just meant . . . like . . . don't worry! Worst-case scenario, he does like you as a person, is all. Clearly."

"Do you know something I don't know? Like about him and Samantha?" I asked.

Katie shook her head. "No. Nothing. I swear."

"You'd tell me if you did, right?" I felt desperate.

"Yes! I promise!" said Katie.

"And you too, Em?" I asked Emma.

Emma nodded solemnly. "I don't know of anything, or anyone, else going on with him. Scout's honor."

I sighed heavily. "I just hope you're right," I whispered.

My dad picked us up for the mall when we were done baking. It was a little tight—the baking shop closed soon, so we'd have to hustle. I was feeling frantic in general, and there was some typical Friday mall traffic, which made it worse. By the time we got into the elevator at the mall, it was a half hour till closing. My dad said he'd circle until we called him to say that we were done.

"Come on, come on!" I urged the creaky elevator.

Everyone else was silent in their nervousness. If we missed the store hours, we'd have to come back in the morning when it opened at ten, and that would be cutting it way too close.

Meanwhile, all I could think about was that I should have played it cooler with Matt at his house. I'm pretty sure guys don't like girls who act like puppy dogs. I think maybe more mystery and reserve is in order. I needed to talk to my sister, Dylan, about it tonight and see what she advised.

I sighed. Emma looked at me as if trying to read my mood. The doors opened, and we burst out into the gallery and ran toward Baker's Hollow. Just as we drew along side it, we heard, "Hey! Hey, Cupcakers!"

My heart lurched. It was Matt! I spun around with a grin, and there he was! Walking with . . . Samantha Perry. My smile instantly faded. Their arms were laden with bags from the crafts store and the hardware store; pipes and Styrofoam pieces protruded from shopping bags. They'd obviously been shopping together for a while. But worst of all, they were eating ice cream!

"Hey!" said Emma, the only one who could find her voice. "Dude, we're late. Can't talk. If this place closes, we're cooked! See ya!"

And she dragged me into Baker's Hollow without me even being conscious of moving my feet. Inside the store, she pulled me down an aisle, with Mia and Katie in hot pursuit. I was speechless, in shock, breathing hard.

"Katie," Emma directed, taking charge like a general. "Go get the sequins. Mia, you'll pay, okay? I am going to talk to Lex for a minute. Come get us when you're all done."

Mia gave me a sympathetic look and squeezed my shoulder, and Katie gave me a quick hug before they took off.

"Okay, deep breaths," instructed Emma. "Just take deep breaths. It's going to be okay. You're going to be fine. It's not what you're thinking, I'm sure."

All I could say was, "They were eating ice cream."

Emma sighed heavily. "Don't worry. I'm sure they just got hungry and . . ."

"But he just ate three cupcakes! He couldn't be hungry!" My voice cracked. I did *not* want to cry in the middle of Baker's Hollow at the mall for goodness' sake!

Emma rolled her eyes. "Oh yes, he could. You don't know how boys eat! It's constant!"

I closed my eyes, but all I could see was the two of them strolling with ice cream in hand. My brain filled out the mental picture, adding in the science fair supplies . . . but then . . .

"Wait! He's doing his *science fair* project with her?! *That's* who's coming over to your *house* tomorrow?!" I wailed, and the tears started, mall or no mall.

I kept crying, and when Mia and Katie returned, the store lights flicked on and off, signaling that Baker's Hollow was getting ready to close.

"Okay, Lex. You've got to stop. What if we see them out there again? You don't want to look upset, remember?" counseled Mia.

She was right. I nodded and gave a big sniff. Katie handed me a wad of paper towels from the test kitchen display. I finally took a bunch of deep breaths.

Emma spoke to me in a firm, low voice. "Pretend you are the CEO of a Fortune 500 company, and something bad has happened that is not your fault, but you need to go out and face the press and deliver the message, okay? Your shareholders are counting on you."

# CHAPTER 6

## Fishing

That night after dinner, I crossed the hall to Dylan's room. She was getting ready to meet friends at the bowling alley, so she was busy, but I barged in, anyway.

"Dyl?

"Mmm-hmm?" She was holding different necklaces up to her neck and studying herself in the mirror with a critical eye.

I flopped onto her bed. "I didn't know you needed the right necklace to go bowling," I teased.

"Which do you like better?" she asked, turning to me. "The green chunky one or the white pebbly one?"

I love it when she asks for my opinion. It is so rare. I gave the question my full attention.

"Shoulders back! Head up!" added Katie.

I took another deep breath. The lights went out, casting us all in shadow. "Okay. I'm ready," I said, pretending to head into a news conference.

"Thanks, Em. Sorry you're in the middle of all this," I said.

"It's okay. It's going to work out fine. Don't worry," she said, shrugging.

"Thanks. I don't think you're right, but thanks, anyway," I said, and squeezed her sideways in a mini hug. (I am not a hugger, so all these hugs were saying a lot about my mental state.)

Katie came back and, silhouetted in the store's doorway, waved us out. "The coast is clear!" she hissed, and Emma and I had to giggle.

We didn't see them again, nor did I go back to the Taylors' that night. We'd be going early in the morning to pick up the cupcakes and bring them to my house for setting up, anyway.

I planned to wait in the car.

"Umm . . . the green. It makes your eyes pop."

"Okay, thanks," she said, setting the green one down on her dresser and fastening the white necklace behind her head.

"No, I said the green!" I hastened to add.

Dylan sighed. "I know. That's why I'm wearing the white. The green is too obvious."

I forgot. Whenever I give my opinion, Dylan does the opposite. "Whatever," I muttered.

"What's up with you?" she asked distractedly.

I went for the jugular; I had to hold her attention somehow. "Matt Taylor has a new girlfriend."

"What?" Dylan spun around to face me.

Despite my misery, I smirked. It had worked.

"Who?" demanded Dylan.

I shrugged. "Some new girl. Samantha Perry."

"Is she pretty?" asked Dylan.

I nodded. "Duh! Yeah. Sporty. Clean-cut. Pretty."

Dylan folded her arms and nodded knowingly. "So just like you."

"I guess. Except the pretty part."

"Shut up. You know you're pretty. Don't act like you don't."

I laughed incredulously. "Seriously? With this carroty-red hair? Pale skin? Freckles? Come on!"

"Alexis Becker, I am not going through this

with you again. You are superpretty and healthy and tall and fit, and it's annoying to act like you're not, so stop. Now, when did they start going out?" Dylan turned back to her dresser and began working on her makeup in the mirror.

I sighed. "Well, I'm not actually sure they're 'going out.'" I made air quotes with my fingers. "But they've been spotted together a lot lately at school, and I know for a fact that she will be at his house tomorrow. Plus, they were at the mall eating ice cream together tonight."

"Wow. So they really *are* going out," agreed Dylan, putting on the maximum amount of mascara she could use without my mom sending her back upstairs to wipe it off.

I sat bolt upright. "Wait, so you *do* think they're really going out?"

Dylan turned from her mirror and looked at me like I had four heads. "What?" She was confused.

"Because of all that stuff I told you. I mean, I was just *assuming* they were going out. But now that you agree, it must be true!" I wailed, and flopped back onto the bed again.

"Stop trashing my bed. I just made it all neat," Dylan said unsympathetically. "I am totally confused. Are they going out or are they not going out?"

"I don't know! I'm asking you!" I shouted.

"How would I know?" Dylan was annoyed. Now she'd never give me advice.

There was only one option to gain her sympathy and help. I hated to do it, but desperate times call for desperate measures; that's what I always say.

I began to cry.

It worked.

"Hey, Lex. Don't cry. It's okay. I'm sure they're just . . . friends. Or something. Don't worry." Dylan rushed to my side and began patting my shoulder. She has always hated it when I cried; even when we were little, it bothered her.

"But I think he's into her. . . . I mean, they're doing their science fair project together, and they were at the library the other day, and tonight they were at the mall, buying all these supplies. . . ." I sniffed for effect.

Dylan took a deep breath. "Okay, wait. So, were they at the mall eating ice cream or shopping for the science fair?"

"Shopping for the science fair *and* eating ice cream," I confirmed with a moan.

Dylan was pensive for a moment. "Okay, so you saw them together at school," she began, ticking off on her fingers.

"At the library," I interjected. I wasn't crying anymore, not now that Dylan was really focused and on my side.

"Okay, even better. The *library*," she emphasized. "Then at the mall buying supplies for the *science fair*, and they *happened to get hungry* and pick up an ice cream. That's not so bad!"

"The ice cream is bad!" I groaned.

"Just hang on a minute. Were they eating the ice cream out of one bowl with two spoons . . . at a table for two? Gazing into each other's eyes?"

I had to laugh, but I swatted Dylan, who laughed too. "No, silly! They were walking with cones," I said.

*"Oh!"* said Dylan in a now-I-see tone of voice. "So, they were walking and eating at the same time. That's not 'having ice cream together at the mall' at all! That's, 'Hey, we're doing other stuff, but I could kind of go for an ice cream right now, what about you, buddy?'"

"Oh, stop. Please." But I was kind of liking Dylan's version of things.

"And why is she going to his house tomorrow?" pressed Dylan.

I stalled a bit, but then I had to admit it. "To work on the science fair project," I mumbled.

"Aha! I rest my case!" said Dylan, standing up and jamming her feet into the awesome rainbow wedge sandals she got with her holiday money from our grandma.

She picked up her purse and looked at me triumphantly. "My work here is done. Now, get out of my room."

"So you don't think they're dating?" I asked, inching to the doorway. I wanted to prolong this conversation as long as I could.

"Nope. Don't worry," said Dylan, flicking off her light switch and pulling her door closed. "But whatever you do, don't mention her to him if you see him. You never want a guy to think you're jealous or even *aware* of the competition."

"Huh. That's what Mia said," I said to Dylan as she clumped down the hall to the stairs.

"See! Mia was always my favorite," Dylan called back up the stairs.

I stood in the upstairs hall for a minute, thinking. "Hey, Dyl?"

*"What?"* she called up in aggravation.

"Don't you need socks?"

"I'm not actually going to *bowl*!" she yelled indignantly. "It would ruin my pedicure!"

I rolled my eyes. Whatever. I can't imagine going

to a bowling alley and not bowling. I mean, what else is there to do, anyway?

That night when my mom came to tuck me in, she asked if everything was all right. And the way she was asking, she meant business.

I wondered if Dylan had mentioned anything to her, but then I quickly waved that thought away. Dylan was too self-involved to share concern for me with our parents unless perhaps if I lay bleeding on the floor somewhere from a wild tiger attack or something.

"I think Matt Taylor likes another girl," I blurted.

My mom sat back in surprise. "Wow! So something really was bothering you!"

"I thought you asked because you could tell!" I said, annoyed to have been tricked into such an easy disclosure.

My mom smiled. "I was just fishing. And it worked."

"Well, whatever. You got lucky," I huffed, folding my arms across my chest and leaning back against my headboard.

She rubbed my leg. "I'm sorry, sweetie. Let's start over. What's this about Matt Taylor?"

I explained everything—the science fair version

and the girlfriend version, just to be fair. My mom bit her lip pensively while I talked.

"So you think she's his girlfriend *why* exactly?" she asked.

"Just because they're together a lot and stuff. And she's pretty?" It sounded lame.

"Well, you're with him a lot and you're pretty!" my mom said cheerfully, as if it was all settled. Now, this was is why my mom is annoying. She just refuses to face the facts sometimes and is always trying to build our self-esteem.

"Mom!" I protested. "I am with Matt Taylor because I happen to be at his house with his sister! Not because he invites me over! There's a big difference," I huffed.

"Oh, right, right. I understand. Well, listen, I think . . . if you really do like Matt, maybe you don't want anything to happen between you two for a while, anyway. Maybe you *are* better off just waiting. Each of you can branch out and meet other people and make other friends, and then later, when you're old enough to really date, you'll be ready and sure!"

"But I don't *want* him to date other people! I want him to date *me*! *Now!*" I wailed.

"You're too young to be dating anyone. Seriously,

at least," my mother pointed out with a sniff.

"Oh, Mom. I just . . . I really, really like him," I said in a small voice.

My mom wrapped her arms across my shoulders, but I stayed stiff. I wasn't giving in so easily again. She talked into my hair. "He *is* adorable. And he's a *nice* boy. And he's certainly familiar and comfortable. He's a perfect first crush. It's puppy love. Someone else will come along. It's not like you're going to *marry* him!"

I pulled out of her hug. "How do you know?!" I demanded. "I might! Ms. Connor at school married the boy she liked in seventh grade!"

My mom smiled. "That's really great, but it's also incredibly rare. People move on, they move away, they change, their interests change. It's just . . . Look. I know it's painful right now, but there are so many fish in the sea! And you are an especially beautiful and rare fish, so many, *many* boy fish will come along and like you! Matt just happens to live in your corner of the aquarium, so you noticed him first! But once you get out on the reef—"

"Mom. Seriously? *Stop!* This is weird. The reef?" *How could my mom be such a dork?* I wondered.

My mom snapped out of it and giggled a little. "Didn't you like my analogy? I thought it was going along swimmingly!" She reached down and tickled me with a laugh.

I had to laugh, but tickling is cheating. "Mom!" I shouted. "Enough! Be serious!"

My mom tried to make a superserious face, but it didn't work, and her trying did actually make me laugh.

"See? I knew you thought it was funny!" said my mom, pointing at me.

I made my face go dead serious. "I'm laughing *at* you, not with you."

My mom made a fake-sad face, and I suddenly thought of Martine and Mrs. Donay and how they were so nice to each other.

I patted my mom on the knee "Sorry, Mom. But seriously. What should I do?"

My mother took a deep breath. "If you really, really like him, then just keep being yourself and try to see him more. That's all I can think of. But don't try too hard. Just enough to keep him interested but still maintain your life and interests."

"Wow! Love advice from Mrs. Becker! Is that how you got Dad?" I teased.

"Yes, if you must know. Men don't like women who play games, though. They like honesty and friendliness. Really, they're just like us, you know?

Except sometimes . . ." My mom lowered her voice and looked over her shoulder, as if to make sure no one could hear her. "Sometimes they can be a little clueless, especially about girls liking them. Just remember that, okay?"

"Okay." I nodded solemnly.

"Matt might not even realize this girl likes him, if she even does like him that way. So there's no need for you to point it out to him and plant the idea in his head. Just keep being yourself and everything will work out, I promise." My mom smoothed my hair back from my forehead and planted a kiss on my head. "Now, it's time for sleep. You have a lot of work to do tomorrow, and that's much more important than any of this boy stuff."

"I know," I agreed.

"For real, Alexis. I don't like to see you too distracted over a boy. You're awfully young for it, and also, you have to learn that there are things that are just as, if not more, important than boys. Such as work, school, your friends and family . . ."

"I know, I know. Please! Remember who you're talking to!" I huffed.

My mom smiled. "Sorry. You're right. Good night, my future CEO. I have total confidence in you. You'll figure this out on your own."

I snuggled down under the covers. "Thanks, Mom."

"Love you, little fish," she said, turning out the light and closing the door.

In the dark I thought about everything my mom and Dylan had said. I knew there was more to life than boys. That was for sure. And deep, deep, deep down inside, where I would never admit it to anyone else because it would sound awful . . . I knew I was pretty. I mean, not a model, like you know who, but definitely strong and smart and healthy and yes, pretty. And I knew it was possible there was nothing more than the science fair between Samantha Perry and Matt, and whatever I did, I shouldn't mention Samantha to Matt. And I knew it was unlikely Matt and I would "end up together," for life or whatever.

But I also knew I just couldn't stand to imagine him with anyone else.

If Matt Taylor was going to have a girlfriend, I wanted her to be *me*.

# CHAPTER 7

## Crunch Time

I woke at seven on Saturday with a pit in my stomach, and it wasn't even about Matt Taylor. Sleep had reset my priorities, and all I could think about was the massive mountain of work we had to do today to get those cupcakes finished and delivered.

I sent a group text to make sure everyone was up and accounted for, and we made a plan for me to go to Emma's for the giant cupcake transfer at eight thirty, and then drop off Mona's order before we picked up Katie and Mia. I had breakfast with my dad and felt much better once I'd had something to eat. Fully charged and ready by eight fifteen, my dad brought me over in our ancient minivan so we could fit all our wares. It wasn't until we pulled into the Taylors' driveway and I spotted an unfamiliar bike that the reality of Samantha spending the day with Matt hit me like a ton of bricks.

"Aren't you going in?" asked my dad, turning to look at me from the front seat.

My face was flushed with anger and jealousy, and my palms were sweating with nerves. "No. I'll just text Emma to say I'm here," I said, furiously punching at my phone.

My dad looked at me for an extra second, making me wonder what my mom had told him about Matt. "Should *I* go in?" he offered.

"Nope. I just sent the text. All set," I huffed. I looked rigidly out the other window, away from the Taylors' house.

A few seconds later Emma came out with a couple of carriers of cupcakes in her hands. My dad pushed the tailgate button to open it and then hopped out to help Emma stow the cupcakes.

"Lex? Any chance of some help?" she called in from the rear.

I thought for a second. "If you bring them to your back door, I'll take them from there, but I'm not going into the house!" I said firmly without turning around.

I could just picture my dad and Emma sharing a look, and it annoyed me.

Angrily, I jerked the door handle to open it, stormed out, and stalked across the driveway to wait outside the back door.

Emma came up behind me. She said in a quiet voice, "Lex, I promise you this is not a romance. Not for Matt, anyway. You should come in just to observe. Trust me. It would make you feel better."

*"No way!"* I protested in a vicious whisper.

Emma sighed. "He's going to wonder where you are. He has the flyers for you to approve."

"I'm sure they're fine. Just bring them. Please."

Emma sighed again and then passed me and went in through the back door. A couple of minutes passed, and the back door opened.

And there was Matt, an arm full of flyers, and the other arm loaded down with two cupcake carriers.

"Hey!" he said. His face lit up when he saw me, I had to admit.

I rearranged my grouchy face into a fake-smile that had no light behind it. "Hey!" I said neutrally.

He looked a little puzzled but kept coming toward me. "I have the flyers. Here. I hope you like them. You check them over while I go put these into your car." He thrust the bunch of flyers at me and went to my car, calling out a greeting to my dad. They began chatting, and I looked over the stack of flyers.

Unfortunately, they were awesome. I really wanted them to stink so I could be mean to him and just tell him to stuff them into the trash, but he had done such a good job. He'd taken our recipe idea and made the page horizontal, with a background in pale yellow, like a lined recipe card. He'd done the recipe in a pretty green handwriting font, so it looked like someone's mom's handwriting, and there was a cute doodle of a cupcake that he must've done himself and scanned. It was just fantastic, beyond what I'd even hoped for. I couldn't contain myself; the CEO in me won out over the lovesick teenager.

"Matt!" I called, wheeling around. "These are *awesome*! Thank you so much!"

Matt turned, and he grinned. "Do you really like them?" he asked shyly.

"Like them? I *love* them!" I cried enthusiastically. Emma came out the door with some more cupcake carriers and then smiled at me.

Matt looked modest. "Well, you guys had the idea. I just put it on paper for you. . . ."

"No way, Matt. These are, like, one of the best things you've ever done. And I love the doodle. You did such a terrific job. Thank you!" I beamed at him, and he beamed back at me.

Just then I heard a voice behind me, "Um, hi? Where can I put these for you guys?"

It was Samantha Perry.

I turned around slowly. She was smiling at me and holding up two huge Tupperware bins filled with frosting. I wanted to die. Or punch her. Or something awful.

Instead, I went into CEO mode again, willing myself not to blush, and for once it worked, thank goodness. "Oh, hi, thank you. You must be Samantha. I'm Alexis," I said politely. "You are so nice to help us. Thanks a million." I sounded like my mom at work, all cool and professional. No one could accuse me of not being nice. Ever. I knew Emma was watching me, but I think my dad was a little clueless, because he was busy arranging carriers in the cargo area of the car.

"Thanks," I said again, taking the Tupperware bins from Samantha's hands and turning so that I could put them into the back of the car.

Matt was standing there with a serious look on his face that I couldn't read, but his eyes were darting back and forth between me and Samantha. I just knew he was comparing us, and I was sure I was losing. Samantha was dressed in white jeans and a cute blue-and-white–striped T-shirt, and had a bouncy ponytail. To her credit, she looked ready to work, not like she was trying to attract a guy in some girlie outfit. I was dressed similarly, and my hair was also in a ponytail. It felt weird. I just wanted the ground to open up and swallow Samantha so Matt and I could continue our lovefest about the flyers.

"You guys sure are busy!" Samantha said nicely.

I tucked the tubs inside the car and turned back to her. "We're lucky. It's a crazy weekend, but it's worth it. And we have these awesome new flyers Matt made us." I couldn't resist throwing that in, just to reinforce my very close relationship with Matt. In any case, it made Matt smile again.

"Can I see?" she asked.

"Sure." I handed the stack to her, and she looked at it admiringly.

"Wow, Matt. These are incredible. I didn't know you did this sort of stuff. Something like this will be great for our project!" said Samantha.

I found myself admiring her work ethic, for thinking of her project right away, and I also felt relieved that she didn't know *everything* about him. (Not that I did, but I *have* known him for many years already and have slept at his house, like, a hundred times. Just saying.)

Matt nodded happily.

"Okay, that's it!" said Emma, loading the last two carriers into the minivan.

I surveyed the scope of what was in there and was amazed it had all fit. I turned to Matt.

"Please let us know what we owe you. These flyers are fantastic. Thank you again." I gave him my sparkliest smile and looked in his eyes for a teeny-weeny extra second, like I was the only fish in the sea.

He smiled back and held my gaze. "Don't worry about it. How about . . . just let me use it in my portfolio, okay?"

The spell was broken, as it often is by money. "Stop. Send us a bill. We can afford it!" I joked, waving at the back of the minivan.

"Good luck!" Samantha said as Emma and I climbed aboard.

"You too!" I said. I then muttered quietly to myself as I shut the door, "On your science project, but nothing else, especially getting Matt!"

"I heard that!" whispered Emma with a devilish grin.

"Good!" I said wickedly.

My dad put the car in reverse and backed out and then drove us at a very stately, cupcake-safe speed to drop Mona's minis at the mall.

"Thanks for not making it weird back there," Emma said quietly as my dad tactfully turned up the radio in the front of the van.

I sighed. "I was going to, trust me. But he really did such a good job. . . ."

Emma was nodding.

"And he is just soooo cute!" I groaned.

Now Emma rolled her eyes.

"Also, I didn't want his last image of me to be crabby. I have my brand to think of," I added, fake-fluffing my hair.

Emma laughed at me. "And what brand is that, missy?"

"Alexis Becker, Inc.! The brand of me!"

"You are too much."

I looked out the window, smiling. But then I pictured Matt and Samantha, spending the day together in that kitchen where I'd spent so much time with him myself, and my smile faded into a thundercloud. By the end of the day, he'd probably be in love with her. But what could be done about it? I had work to do.

We dropped off Mona's minis, picked up Katie and Mia, and then we set up shop in my kitchen. It was like a full-on assembly line. All the naked cupcakes sat in their carriers with the lids off, waiting to be jazzed up with frosting and then re-covered for delivery. I was thrilled to see it since there really is such a thing as economy of scale—when we buy a lot of flour or eggs or sugar at once, it *is* cheaper, so our unit cost (the cost per cupcake) goes down. All this makes my heart beat a little faster in happiness.

First, we worked through the two dozen pink frilly cupcakes for Libby's birthday party. They were really delicious in the end: angel food cake—moist and dense and tinted pink—with pink marshmallow cream frosting that Mia piped on in waves so it looked like a tutu on top of the cupcake. They were so delicious and beautiful that we took a photo, and I e-mailed it to myself to file for future use. (As an interesting side note, Katie told me that angel food cake is very low in fat. It's healthy enough that I almost could have used it as my cake for the science fair cupcakes. Good to know!)

Next, we did the mud cakes for Sawyer's birthday. These were easy since they didn't have to look fancy—just tasty. The chocolate cakes had a fudgy pudding-like frosting, and we rolled the edges in crushed Oreos. It was too much chocolate for me, but it did look appealingly (if you were a little boy) like mud, and they were dense and moist and tasty. Those boys would surely have crashes after eating those party cupcakes and need naps! They were definitely *not* science fair caliber!

The hygienist's cupcakes were easy—plain yellow cake with pale yellow frosting (the baby shower had a rubber ducky theme; the client had purchased tiny rubber duckies in bulk and would be topping the cupcakes with them herself).

Finally, we set to work on Martine's cupcakes. There were a lot of them, and we had to get the two kinds of base frosting on and do the sequin cupcakes first, while the frosting set a while for the ones getting the fondant toppers (they'd need something kind of firm to sink into, so they didn't just slide off).

The only problem was the sequins weren't sticking.

"I think we'll need these to sit awhile too," said Mia.

"Let's load up the carriers while we're waiting," suggested Emma.

"Great idea," I agreed.

"Actually, I'll put them right into the car," added Emma.

We set to work, neatening up any dribbled frosting, snapping the tops back onto their carriers, and then putting them by the back door, where Emma was ferrying them out to the minivan.

"How are we doing on time?" asked Katie.

I looked at my watch. "Yikes. The pink cupcakes need to be at the Murrays' house in ten minutes! And Sawyer's cupcakes in half an hour. The hygienist's can be anytime, but Martine's need to be at her house in an hour. We're going to have to do two trips. Dad!" I called.

"In here!" He was working at his desk in the den. I scurried in and asked urgently if he would be able to drive us over to the three drop-offs right this very minute. My mom was away at a conference for the weekend, and Dylan was babysitting at the O'Haras' for the whole day.

My dad was kind of bummed to leave his work, but he agreed, luckily, and went to find his shoes.

Back in the kitchen, things were still humming along.

Katie was testing to see if the frosting was ready to hold the fondant instruments yet, but they kept sliding off. "Aargh! This is so frustrating. Maybe we didn't make the frosting thick enough?" she wondered aloud.

"Here, let me see," said Mia.

"Guys, I'll leave you two on that while Emma and I deliver these cupcakes, and then we'll circle back to get them, okay?" I asked.

"Good idea," agreed Mia.

My dad had the minivan running when Emma and I ran out and hopped in.

"Wait! The flyers!" I cried, and I dashed back in to get them. No point in Matt doing all that work and us paying for them if no one would ever see them. I returned to the car, panting, and now beginning to panic about the time.

"Okay, let's hit the road!" I said urgently.

"How about a 'please'?" grumbled my dad, reversing the car. "What am I, Jeeves the Chauffeur?"

"Sorry, Dad. Please?"

He harrumphed, and Emma and I exchanged nervous and guilty smiles. My dad is always such a good sport, so if I was annoying him, it wasn't a good thing.

"Okay, so now where to?" he asked, fiddling with his seat belt. I told him the Murrays' address, and we set out.

As we rode along I had a thought. "Em, we don't want to look like we're in a rush when we get there, you know?"

Emma nodded. "Right. We need to be cool as cucumbers."

"We never want a client to think we're too busy or not giving them our full attention."

"Got it!" agreed Emma, and we fist-bumped professionally.

I glanced at my dad in the rearview mirror and saw that he was smiling. Phew.

We reached the Murrays' house in good time, and Emma and I quickly unloaded the car but brought the pink cupcakes into the kitchen at a stately pace. Libby, the birthday girl, was dressed in a pink tutu, and Emma and I exchanged a knowing look of pleasure. These cupcakes would be a hit. Besides being delicious, the pink tutu effect of the frosting would be ideal for this ballerina birthday girl!

We made a little small talk with Mrs. Murray, and then she paid us, and we made arrangements to pick up the carriers later in the week if she would just leave them on her back step. With a happy wave, as if we had all the time in the world, Emma and I stepped graciously out the back door and . . . flat-out sprinted to the van!

"Okay, Jeeves!" I teased my dad. "Now we're going to One Hundred Lily Pond Lane!" I resisted the urge to add, "And step on it!"

My dad gave a little salute, and we were off.

I couldn't stop looking at my watch; we were starting to cut it a little close.

"Should we call the others and see how it's going?" I asked Emma.

She nodded and called Mia on her phone.

I listened to Emma's side of the conversation in relief. Things were sticking, the cupcakes looked good, and it was going to be fine. Yay! We had this!

We reached the Reeses' house, and this time we put just a teeny bit more spring in our step and were out the door in five minutes instead of ten. Once again, we hit the road, and now Emma and I were on a roll. The next drop-off at the hygienist's went superfast, and back in the car, we were feeling maybe a little too confident.

"We should really drum up more business," I was saying.

"Totally! We can *easily* do multiple orders a day on the weekends. I think we've just gotten really efficient!" agreed Emma.

But suddenly, there started to be this really bad burning smell. I wrinkled my nose and looked out the window for the source of the odor. Was someone burning tires in their yard? Was there a new factory in town? Then I looked out the rear window.

"Dad! There's smoke billowing out the back of the car!" I yelled.

"What?" he replied in a panic, looking back and then pulling over. "Oh no! It's the fuel injector. Your mom was supposed to take it to get fixed last week. . . . Oh, brother!"

Emma and I stared at each other, totally shocked. I didn't dare say anything as my dad jumped out of the car, fuming, and lifted the hood of the van to see inside. (Not like that would help because he knows zero about cars, anyway.)

"What are we going to do if we can't drive this car?" I asked Emma in a panicked whisper.

"Don't worry. I'll get us a ride. My parents are at a wedding shower out of town, but maybe I can get Sam, and he can at least go get Martine's cupcakes." She punched the numbers on her phone and made wide eyes at me as it rang and no one picked up. Finally, she hung up. "He's not answering. Let me try our home number, though it's unlikely anyone will ever answer that."

Meanwhile, my dad was calling AAA on his phone to see what he should do. I wrung my hands together and was thrilled when someone picked up Emma's call.

"Matt?" she said, making wide eyes at me again.

She proceeded to explain our situation and ask where Sam was.

"Oh no!" she said. I made a horrified face and she mouthed, *Sam's at work—picked up a shift today.*

But then Matt was saying something, and Emma looked right into my eyes as she listened. "I don't know. . . . That's awfully nice. I know, it's not really out of the way. I . . . Let me check with Alexis. Hang on."

She muted her phone and stared at me for a minute. "No one else in my family is able to drive, but Samantha Perry's dad is on his way to get her. He can pass by your house, get the cupcakes, and bring them to Martine's on his way to my house, and we can meet him there. What do you want me to say? We could try Mia's parents or Katie's mom, but it's a gamble, and we might lose this ride."

I felt stricken. "Seriously?" I sat for a second with my forehead in my hands. Then I stuck my head out the window. "Dad? Sorry to bug you, but should we find another ride for the rest of the cupcakes?"

"Yes!" he barked.

I ducked my head back into the car.

"Business first, Lex?" Emma said gently.

"Oh, whatever. Fine," I grumbled. "And thanks."

And then I put my hands over my ears as Emma made the rest of the arrangements.

# CHAPTER 8

## Saved!

Emma and I decided to walk to the Donays' house, figuring we stood a chance of getting there around when Mr. Perry arrived with the cupcakes. I felt awful leaving my dad on the side of the road, but he was in such a foul mood, it was probably better we weren't there to witness it.

Emma called Katie and Mia, and luckily, they were almost finished setting the decorations on top of the cakes. They were going to start packing everything up and getting ready for the pickup right away. Emma said they should ask Mr. Perry if they could please ride along in his car with him, so at least they'd be there, just in case we couldn't walk there fast enough.

That finished, and after promising my dad we'd

call him once we'd gotten to the Donays' house, we set out on what would be a twenty-five-minute walk.

I was so stressed, I could hardly speak.

It was bad enough my family's car had broken down and let us all down, and I had ditched my dad after all he'd done for us this weekend already, and we'd bitten off more than we could chew, work-wise, but to have to accept the help of someone who is basically my rival, well . . . it was all just too much. I sighed as we marched up the busy four-lane road, cars whizzing by us. It wasn't exactly a highway, but it wasn't a place many pedestrians ventured, either.

Emma tried to cheer me up at first by talking business, of course, but I was too distraught to chat. Luckily, she had remembered to grab the flyers, at least, before we left the minivan, so that hadn't been a total loss.

"Hey, these things came out great, don't you think?" she said cheerily.

"I wish I'd worn better shoes," I muttered, refusing to be cheered.

"Oh, I know." Emma sighed. "I wish I had on my sneakers. Or my fluffy slippers," she joked. We were silent for another block.

"Samantha's actually really nice," said Emma after a bit. "And—"

I raised my hand, palm out, for her to stop. "Please." I shook my head and looked at the ground.

Emma sighed heavily, and we walked another block. Then she burst out, "All I was going to say is, I don't think he likes her like that. That's all!"

"Hmph!" I said with a humorless laugh.

"I'm serious, Lex. I watched them together this morning, and while I do think *she* might have the teeniest crush on *him*, I really don't think he likes her back."

"Why?" I asked. I didn't mind us talking *that* much if this was to be the topic.

Encouraged, Emma turned to me as we walked. "See, she's really chatty and upbeat and giggly with him, and he is just his plain self. Now, that could just be how boys are, but I have to say, I've seen how Matt is with *you*, and honestly, Lex, he can't stop grinning when you're around."

A tiny smile lifted the corners of my lips—just the teensiest bit. "Really? Go on."

"I swear. I don't think he's into her."

"No, I mean, how is he with me?"

Emma tilted her head and gave it her full consideration. "Well, he's himself but good. Better. Like, his best self. And he's nice and friendly and never grumpy or snarky, and he's willing to do stuff for us, like the flyers and whatever. . . ."

"We pay him!" I said, scowling now.

Emma stopped and threw her hands into the air as she looked at me. "Alexis Becker, please! Do you honestly think he cares about the money? He does it so he can hang out with you. I'm sure of it!"

"Hmm, well, maybe I'm just his starter person. He's practicing on me to get ready for a real girlfriend."

"Oh, Alexis, you are impossible."

Now I'd succeeded in putting Emma in a bad mood. I was kind of relieved she was now cranky too, because I was sick of her attempts to cheer me up, but after we walked another block, I felt bad. There was no need for me to burst her bubble just because I was so miserable.

So I said, "I'm sorry, Emma. It's just—"

"It's fine, Alexis. Whatever. I shouldn't get involved, anyway. It really has nothing to do with me, and it's probably better if we keep it that way."

"I'm sorry," I said lamely.

She shrugged and then squinted at her phone. "Only three more blocks if we cut through the playground."

I agreed, and we veered off and onto the grass of the park surrounding the playground. The park was busy because it was a nice weekend, so I don't know how I spotted her, but suddenly I saw someone who looked familiar, sitting on a bench.

"Hey." I nudged Emma. "Isn't that Martine Donay over there, all by herself?"

Emma looked. "I think you're right. She looks miserable! What do you think she's doing over there?"

We stared at each other for a split second, unsure. Emma checked the time on her watch. "Her party's soon. She should be getting ready right now."

"Should we go over there?"

Emma shrugged nervously. "We might be late if we do."

"Well, without her there's no party! Come on. Let's go!"

We walked over to where Martine sat on a bench, her knees pulled up in front of her, her arms wrapped around them.

"Martine?" I called tentatively.

She looked up, and her eyes were tear streaked, and her heavy mascara was running.

"Hey! What's the matter?" I said, rushing now to her side. I sat next to her on the bench. She looked as if she had dressed for the party already, because although she was wearing her normal outfit of ripped black jeans and three layers of T-shirts all cut up and held together with leather cords and safety pins, her hair was . . . punkier than usual—black and completely vertical. She had on tons of jangly chains and earrings.

She looked shocked to see us, and sniffed away her tears and dabbed at her eyes with the corner of a black bandanna, trying to look natural, like she hadn't been crying. "Oh, hey," she said quietly.

"What's wrong, Martine?" Emma asked kindly. "Isn't it almost time for your party?"

Martine gave a dark laugh. "*My* party? *My* party? Ha! As if!"

Emma and I exchanged a glance. "Um, whose party is it?" I asked.

Martine gave an angry sigh. "My mother's! That's who! I never wanted anything to do with a sweet sixteen, and she bullied me into it, and now it's a mess, and I am not going!"

"Why is it a mess?" I asked.

"Ack!" Martine waved her hand in frustration. "Just . . . everything."

Emma and I looked at each other again. Now Emma asked, "Like what?"

Martine said, "For starters, she tried to insist that I wear a skirt! A skirt! Me! Can you imagine?"

We shook our heads simultaneously.

"Then she insisted on all these party foods from her favorite takeout place, like finger sandwiches! And deviled eggs! It's like we're at a ladies' tea or something!"

"Oh. Yeah. That's, um . . ." I happen to love tea sandwiches and deviled eggs, so I was the wrong person to handle this. I looked beseechingly at Emma.

Emma got the hint. "Well . . . maybe people will think it's ironic or something. Like a joke?"

"She's the joke!" Martine snorted.

I had to step in. "I have to say, there are certain foods everyone loves, and tea sandwiches and deviled eggs are two of them. . . ."

"And pigs in a blanket?" guessed Emma. "Is she serving those?"

Martine rolled her eyes and nodded sadly.

"Oh, well, people just go nuts for those. Trust me!" said Emma. "Even cool people!"

I added, "And people will be hungry, with all that dancing and thrashing around and whatnot. I think you'll be surprised to see how fast the food goes. I mean, you're having boys, right?"

Martine nodded again.

Emma looked at Martine knowingly. "That food will fly."

"Anyway, what did you want to serve? I mean, is there such a thing as punk food?" I asked.

Martine sighed. "Not really, I guess. I just hate for her to get everything her way."

"Well, at least the cupcakes are your way!" I said brightly.

Martine frowned thoughtfully. "Yeah. I just wish we could have done the tattoo ones."

"I know, but it might have been a little weird, everyone eating your name, you know?" I giggled, and then so did Martine.

"Maybe," she said.

I glanced at Emma. We'd gotten a foothold!

"And speaking of cupcakes . . . ," said Emma.

"Oh yes, people love cupcakes! Trust us!" I said, smiling encouragingly.

"No, I mean . . ." Emma wiggled her phone meaningfully at me.

"Oh, right! Yeah. We've got to go meet the cupcakes at your house. They're getting dropped off, like, now-ish. . . ."

"Come with us. Let's all walk over together," suggested Emma.

Martine sighed heavily. "Okay. I guess."

"Come on! You can't miss your own sweet sixteen! Just imagine if people started skipping their own sweet sixteens because their moms were annoying them! There would never be a single birthday girl at her own party. Right?" Emma said.

Martine smiled. "You're right."

"The best thing to do is go and have a blast. Don't even think about your mom. Also, finger sandwiches and deviled eggs aren't a reflection on you. People will probably assume the caterer just brought them and whatever. They'll go over really well. Trust me. I have three brothers," Emma said, rolling her eyes.

"Right," said Martine. "Actually, I know your brother Matt. From school."

"Oh yeah. Right," said Emma, nodding. "Good old Matt," she joked, looking sideways at me.

I rolled my eyes.

Martine was thinking. "Wait, now something reminds me . . . Oh, yeah. One of my guests asked if she could bring him as a date to the party! That's what!"

A huge pit opened inside my stomach. "Oh really?" I said supercasually, but inside I was already dying a slow death. "Um, who?"

I braced myself for the answer, even though it was as inevitable as could be.

"Samantha Perry?" said Martine, cocking her head. "Do you know her?"

"Oh, brother!" said Emma, smacking her forehead. "Here we go!"

"Interesting. Yes, we sort of know her," I said. We were almost at Martine's, and I knew who would be waiting there for us: Samantha Perry.

"Hey!" said Emma, eager to change the subject. "It's funny—I mean, not funny ha-ha but funny odd—that you are in a fight with your mom, you know? Because, um, I hope you won't be offended that we discussed this or whatever, but . . . we all thought it was cool how well you got along with your mom when we were at your house, you know?"

"Oh really?" said Martine, giving it some consideration. "That *is* funny."

My emotions were so riled up by her news about Samantha and Matt attending her party, I could hardly focus on what Martine was saying. It was all I could do not to burst into tears myself.

*Of all the crazy coincidences,* I thought bitterly. Here I am killing myself to get cupcakes for Matt and Samantha to enjoy together at a party I am not invited to. I think I'll go back to that park bench.

Martine went on. "Anyway, I guess it's true. My mom and I do get along pretty well. I mean, she was really young when she had me, so we're almost more like sisters sometimes." She shrugged.

"It's pretty cool that she doesn't give you a hard time about your look," said Emma.

Martine laughed as we rounded the corner to her street. "She did at first, but then she decided it was a phase and she should just ignore it. It's only on big occasions like this when it becomes a problem for her. She's kind of old-fashioned and French that way. You know, look your best all the time, et cetera. The funny thing is, she was a punk when she was a teenager. She was even at the real CBGB club once—can you believe it? And she had a tattoo, but she got it removed and so . . ."

I wasn't even listening, really, even though Martine's news was interesting. Because up ahead, I could see a station wagon pulled up in front of Martine's house and a bunch of people unloading stuff and putting it into the back of Mrs. Donay's SUV, parked just ahead of it. Sure enough, there were Mia and Katie and an unfamiliar dad and . . . Samantha Perry and Matt.

Luckily, Emma was reacting to Martine's

disclosure, so Martine didn't notice when I stopped dead in my tracks. I couldn't go on. I could not face Sam and Matt. I spluttered, "I'll . . . meet you after, okay, Emma? I'll just go back to the park and wait."

Emma's jaw dropped as she turned to stare at me. Martine looked at me in confusion.

"What? Why?" she asked.

"I just . . . There's some stuff . . ."

"Alexis Becker!" hissed Emma. "Business first! Let's go!"

Ugh! What a cheap shot, using my own motto on me.

I stood there, paralyzed between what I wanted to do (flee) and what I knew I should do (go and face the music).

Then Martine said, "Oh! There's your brother, Emma. And there's Samantha! He's such a nice guy. . . ."

My soul felt crushed. I felt tears brimming, so I quickly put my head down so no one could see them. I knew what was coming next: something about what a cute couple they made or how she knew they'd always be right for each other. But what came next shocked me.

"It's too bad he turned her down about the party."

"What?" My head snapped up, and I turned to look at Martine.

"Listen, thanks for cheering me up," said Martine, not hearing my question. "I think I'd better run. I can't wait to taste those cupcakes! I hope I see you all soon!" She blew us kisses as she trotted ahead to her brick walkway.

"See?" Emma said smugly.

I shook my head in disbelief. "It still doesn't mean . . ."

"Just stop it, Alexis. It means exactly what it sounds like it means. Now, come on! March!" And she stalked off ahead of me.

I stood there for a minute, watching from a safe distance as people milled around the back of the cars. Could it be true? Could it be that Matt doesn't like Samantha Perry like that? I guess there was only one way to find out.

I set out again, closing the gap between me and Matt with each step.

# CHAPTER 9

## Closing the Loop

I drew up alongside Mia and Katie first. "Hey," I said quietly.

"Lexi! You made it!" squealed Kate, hugging me in a tight neck squeeze.

"I cannot believe we pulled this off," Mia mumbled into my ear.

"I know," I whispered back. "Close call."

"Too close," Mia admitted, nodding. "Let me introduce you to Mr. Perry."

"Oh . . . I . . ." But it was too late.

"Mr. Perry, here is our CEO, Alexis Becker! She walked all the way from her broken-down car to make it here!"

I turned, and there was Mr. Perry. "Nice to meet you," I said, sticking out my hand and automatically giving him a big smile, like I was a robot.

He had a warm, easy grin, and a big hand. "I am very impressed by this outfit you're running, Ms. Becker! You are a titan of industry! I wish I could get my kids to work half as hard," he said, glancing at Samantha, who was chatting with Matt.

"Oh well," I said, waving my hand airily. "When you love what you do . . ." (I'd heard someone say that in a movie once and had been dying to use it for ages.)

Mr. Perry laughed kindly. "Yes. True."

"Thank you so much for helping us. We were really in a jam," I said. "You were like . . . divine intervention!"

"Right place, right time," he said, shaking his head. "It was no problem at all."

He put his hands on his hips and surveyed his empty cargo area. "I guess that's it. Is there anyplace I can take you girls?"

"Oh. Um, that's so nice of you, but you've done more than enough. We really appreciate it. We owe you a free batch of cupcakes!" I said.

He laughed. "You don't owe me anything! But I will take one of those flyers so I can share it with my wife. I'm sure we can dream up a reason to order some!"

"They're perfect for any occasion! Completely customizable, and now with healthy options too!" I joked in my best salesperson voice as I handed him one of Matt's flyers.

"Cute!" he said, looking at it.

"Matt made them," I said.

He looked at it again and then looked over at Matt appraisingly. "Impressive again. Well, good luck to the Cupcake Club. It was a pleasure meeting you all. Samantha! Ready?"

As they pulled away I suddenly got too nervous to talk to Matt. "I'm just going to run up and check in with Mrs. Donay, okay?" I announced, starting up the walk.

"We'll wait here!" called Mia.

I reached the front door, which was open, and I drummed it with my fingers. "Hello?" I called.

I ventured into the house. I figured someone would be in the kitchen.

As I rounded the corner through the dining room, I called, "Hello? Mrs. Donay?" and I spied Martine and her mom in the kitchen in a big hug.

They pulled apart and smiled at me.

"Alexis! Thank you for bringing my Martini back!" joked Mrs. Donay.

"Oh, she came back on her own," I said,

laughing. "She couldn't wait to taste our cupcakes!"

"The cupcakes look great, Alexis. Thank you so much! And did you see the one the girls did for me?" said Martine, smiling.

"No. What is it?"

"The tattoo one with my name on it. Just one of them—just for me."

I smiled back. "Great idea. I'm glad you like it."

"Alexis, I owe you money!" said Mrs. Donay.

"Oh, I'm not here to collect. You can pay me anytime. I just wanted to say if you could please leave the carriers on your porch when you're finished, we will swing by and grab them tomorrow, okay?"

"Still," said Mrs. Donay, "I have it right here." She handed me an envelope, and I thanked her.

"I hope you have a smashing time at the party!" I said. "Thanks so much for hiring us. "*Oh!* And have a flyer!" I left one on their counter, and they both remarked on how good it was.

"Matt Taylor did it," I said.

Martine smiled. "He's a good guy."

I nodded in agreement. "Well, I'd better go. Have fun!"

We called out our good-byes as I jogged back out of the house.

Outside, I knew the Cupcakers were waiting for me, but I was surprised to see that Matt was still there too.

"All set?" asked Emma.

"Yup." I patted my pocket, which made a crinkly sound from the envelope. I didn't dare meet Matt's eyes, so I looked at the Cupcake girls.

"Where to?" I asked.

"We're all going to my house," Emma said firmly. "For a nice cool drink and a snack and some couch time."

"Phew, we've earned it!" agreed Katie.

"Hey, it's my house too," said Matt.

"So, are you coming?" said Emma as we set off.

"That depends. Do you have any more cupcakes?" joked Matt.

Emma rolled her eyes.

Matt fell into step beside me as we walked, and I was tongue-tied.

"How's your science project going?" he asked.

I knew I was blushing from the attention, so I kept my eyes on the sidewalk below me. "I'm in good shape. Tomorrow I need to do my flyers. I have all the info written up, but I'm going to just do a folding thing, with columns. . . ."

"I'll help you!" offered Matt.

I snapped my head up to look at him, blushing even harder now. "What about your flyers?"

"Oh," he said, waving his hand. "We don't need flyers. That would be overkill. We're doing poster boards. Ours is pretty self-explanatory. It's about closed loops in computing. We're doing models with PVC piping."

"Oh. Wow. Um. That's interesting?" I said, thinking the opposite.

Matt laughed. "No, it's not. It was Samantha's idea. She asked me to be her partner." He shrugged. "And since no one else had asked me, I just said yes."

I glanced at him, but he was looking away, and now *his* cheeks seemed a bit pink.

Suddenly, I found my footing. "So, are you saying you might have been available to help out on a cupcake project if only I'd asked?" I said, trying to sound casual.

Matt looked over at me. "Yes. That's exactly what I'm saying."

"Oh," I said, my cheeks flaming. "Well. Who knew?"

Back at the Taylors' house, the first thing I did was call my dad. He was in a much better mood than when I had left him earlier. The tow truck had come, and the cost of the tow was covered by AAA. Then it turned out that the fuel injector was an easy and inexpensive fix; he'd be picking it up with my mom first thing Monday. Now he was planted in front of the TV, watching golf and thawing a turkey meat loaf my mom had left for dinner, so all was right with the world for him. I thanked him profusely for helping us and promised to bake him a dozen cupcakes that he could eat before my mom came home and threw them away.

With that all settled, I turned my attention to my friends, and we had a blast. There was a tray of angel food cupcakes we'd left behind this morning ("Samantha left these on purpose! "Sabotage!" I joked to Emma, but she just rolled her eyes, refusing to bite), so Katie quickly whipped up some of that insane marshmallow frosting, and we all had a delicious snack.

Then we plopped onto the couch in the Taylors' TV room, and Matt invited over his friends Joe Proctor and Ken Dreher, and we all hung out and watched a movie, and then it was time for everyone to go home.

Mia's stepdad came to get her, and he also offered to drive me home.

At home, I showered and headed downstairs

to set the table and see what I could do to help with dinner. Dylan had arrived home from babysitting, and I filled her in on everything that had happened.

"Wow!" She couldn't believe it. "That's intense! Making all those deadlines, the car breaking down, finding Martine in the park, the Samantha Perry factor. Wow! Good for you!" She actually seemed pleased for me.

"Thanks," I said.

Dylan nibbled on a carrot stick thoughtfully. "You know, it is possible you and Matt could end up together, in the end. I mean, it is rare, but it does happen."

I shrugged. "Who knows? I'm just glad that for now, he's not into Samantha Perry."

"The boy I had a crush on when I was your age. . . . Let's just say things did not turn out well for us," said Dylan.

"Who?"

"Remember Alex MacPhearson?"

"How could I forget? You were carving that guy's initials into everything at one point! Remember how you got in trouble for the one on Grandma's tree?"

Dylan hid her face in her hands as I laughed.

"Oh, it is so mortifying to think of it now. It was total puppy love, and he wound up being such a jerk!"

"Right. Something with a dance, or what was it?"

My dad came out of the pantry then and started casually fiddling with the food for dinner, warming up the mashed potatoes and steaming the green beans and acting like he wasn't listening. Dylan's back was to him, so I don't know if she realized she had an audience. Anyway, she was so into her story, she probably wouldn't have cared.

"I loved him to death, and we were supposed to go to the dance together, but then Sandy Lamont asked him and he went with her and left me at home, all dressed up and ready. The next day, when my friends called him on it, he was like, 'Uh, what? My mom arranged the ride for me. I thought we were meeting at the dance?' Duh! I was mortified! I couldn't stand him after that."

"Oh, I remember that night. That was bad," I agreed.

My dad poured our milk and brought the glasses to the table. He had a little smile on his face. "You girls should try to think of the boy's perspective sometimes too, you know," he said. "What he said was probably true. Maybe the two moms were best friends or something, and they set it up that way."

"Well, he was spineless to go along with it!" snapped Dylan.

"He was *twelve*!" my dad said with a laugh. "Twelve-year-old boys have no say! You know, a lot of the time, girls are blowing these simple events up into these big romantic outings, and boys just don't see things that way."

I smiled. "So, how *do* boys see it?" I knew he was dying to tell us.

He began, "It goes something like this: 'Oh, there's a dance? Do I have to take a shower? Okay, then I'm not going. Fine, whatever, I guess I do have to take a shower, anyway. I'll go. Wait, I have to wear a shirt with a collar? Then I'm not going. Oh, all my friends are going so I have nothing else to do? Okay. I guess I'll go. But there's a big NBA game on then, so I'm not going. Well, what *kind* of snacks will they have at the dance? Oh, Mom, fine! I'll go for five minutes, but I am not riding with that lunatic girl just because her mom is your friend. That girl won't leave me alone! It's weird! What? What do you mean she's in the driveway? I hate you! I am never doing this again. You're ruining my life!' And then he slams the door and goes to the dance with Sandy Lamont," my dad said, grinning.

Dylan and I stared at him, openmouthed.

"What were you, a *boy* once or something?" Dylan said finally.

My dad grinned again and nodded. "And meanwhile, all the girls are thinking—I mean, nothing personal—but you watch so many movies and listen to so many songs, you all have these love stories floating around in your heads, and you're thinking, 'Tonight's the night! The moon is full, I'm wearing my good luck charm, I washed my hair with eggs so it will shine. . . ."

"Dad!" I swatted him, and he laughed and continued.

"And maybe Archie MacFulcrum will be there and see me and take me in his arms. . . ."

"It was Alex MacPhearson, Dad!" cried Dylan, laughing.

"Right, him too," joked my dad. "And anyway, you're all imagining this ball with the glass slipper and the kiss at midnight and trust me, the boys *are not*."

"Wow," I said. "Are you finished?"

"So, what are they imagining, then?" asked Dylan.

My dad spun on his heel. "Food. Mostly food. Maybe decent music. Seeing their friends so they can rag on one another. And anything beyond that is sports or their hobby or whatever it is they're into. Romance is dead last. Sorry."

Dylan and I looked at each other.

"Okaaaay . . . so what you're saying is, if we want to catch a guy, we need to offer good food and be sporty and have cool hobbies?" she said.

"Pretty much. But even then it will take a while," he said with a nod, fixing our plates.

"Well, at least you've got it all . . . ," said Dylan, turning to me.

"Me? What do you mean?"

"You're sporty, and you make tons of good food, and you have that whole business hobby."

"But I don't do any of that in order to get *boys*!" I protested.

"Bingo!" said my dad, putting our plates on the table. "That's the attitude I'm looking for! Now, let's eat."

That night in bed I thought about the day and everything my dad had said, and it kind of made sense, I had to admit. I need to just live my life and not think about trying to "get" Matt or whatever.

Because Matt is not thinking about how to "get" me. We need to just have fun with our lives and work hard, and anything else that happens is just the icing on the (cup)cake!

# CHAPTER 10

## Seal of Approval

The science fair was a pretty big event in the end. There were a hundred entries, each with its own table and at least one person manning it. There were ten judges, and the prizes were cash, and they were sizable. Also, the winner would get to put a seal on their project saying COUNTY SCIENCE FAIR GRAND-PRIZE WINNER, with the year and everything.

I wanted to win.

Setting up started early that morning, and I was nervous. The Cupcakers had helped me the day before with baking the junky boxed-mix cupcakes with canned frosting and then Katie's healthy cakes with the dark chocolate glaze. The healthy cupcakes looked and smelled delicious, and the boxed-mix cakes smelled really artificial and chemical. Gross.

My flyers looked awesome too. Matt had done them for me using the real calorie count label, like the one you find on the back of a food or drink product, just as I'd imagined. He did one for the "fake" cakes and one for the healthy cakes—with and without frosting. The differences were significant. Then I did an overview on childhood obesity and the rise of diabetes, with lots of scary statistics and what we can all do to make healthier choices. I took my mom's advice and bought party tablecloths to drape over my table. They were an oversize blue-and-white gingham, with matching plates, cups, and napkins. The cupcake wrappers on the healthy cakes were silver foil, so it all looked good together, while the ones on the boxed-mix cakes were an ugly pale yellow. Then I bought two dozen blue-and-white helium balloons and tied them to the corners of my table, so people could see them from anywhere in the room. It was eye-catching, for sure.

My friends took turns handing out flyers for me as I fielded questions about my thesis ("Cupcakes Can Be Good for You!") and gave out samples. I was holding back twelve cupcakes of each kind for the judges (two were extra, just to be safe), so I cut the other few dozen into slices so people could have a nibble.

Every single person made a face after they tried the boxed-mix cupcakes, I was happy to see. I tried to be diplomatic, saying, "Look, people are busy, we rush for the mix, figuring it's just this once. But kids eat them 'just this once,' like, twenty or thirty times a year. Real cupcakes don't take long at all, and there's no reason not to make them taste good, even if they are healthy." People were nodding, and I have to admit, I was glad I'd thought to bring the remainder of the promotional flyers Matt had made for us. I handed out every last one of them.

I had seen Matt and Samantha when we were all let into the gymnasium, but their table was at the opposite end from me. By midmorning, the Cupcakers went to tour the other exhibits, and suddenly, Matt appeared and inspected everything. "Looking good, Alexis. Even your outfit!"

I'd worn blue pants, a white top, blue sneakers, and a blue-and-white gingham apron. I blushed and thanked him.

"You look ready to go on QVC and sell your wares!" he said.

"Hey, don't joke! That's my goal!" I said with a grin. "How's it going at your end?"

"Pretty good. Our thing is a little boring. I mean, people get it and say nice things, but we don't have any treats like this." He gestured to the cupcakes.

"Want one?" I asked.

"From which platter?" he said.

I shrugged. "One from each?"

"Thanks!"

He gobbled them down as he stood there, and when he had finished, I said, "Which kind did you like better?"

"Wait, were they different?" he asked.

My heart dropped. "Couldn't you tell? It's the whole point of the—"

"Kidding!" he said, breaking into a grin. "The fake one is gross. Way too sugary. But let me know if you have any left over, anyway. I'm sure I could force some down."

I giggled and then poured him a cup of water from my pitcher to wash down the cupcakes. "Very funny!" I singsonged.

And then suddenly he let out a loud burp.

"You are too gross," I said, laughing and shaking my head sadly at the same time. "Just when I think . . ."

"What?" he asked, suddenly all serious. "Just when you think what?"

There was a split second of tension as I debated whether I should tell him what I really thought, but I chickened out. *Why go there here and now,* I thought. *Save it for another day.*

"Just when I think the judges are coming to see me! Now scram!" I cried, shooing him away.

I wasn't kidding. The group of judges had just rounded the corner of my aisle, and I was the second table. I hastened to straighten everything up, wiping crumbs off the table into a napkin, throwing away discarded paper cups and plates, shuffling my flyers to put the freshest one on top and squaring off the pile, and fluffing my balloons. I was in go mode and wanted everything perfect. I did adore Matt, but it was all about my work now.

I freshened the platter of cupcakes and spun it so the most delectable-looking ones were on the outside. Then I finger-brushed my hair, nervously poured myself some water and had a quick cool drink, and then they were there!

I introduced myself and gave my two-minute presentation. I offered cupcake samples to everyone, and they graciously took them, with some people trying bites right then, and some not. (*How could you not?* I wondered.) They asked some hard questions, I answered pretty thoroughly, they nodded and made all kinds of notes on their clipboards, and then they were off to the next table.

Suddenly, the Cupcakers were swarming around me.

"Lex! How did it go?" Katie asked.

"We watched from afar. We didn't want to come back and interrupt you," Emma said.

"You looked superpro!" Mia cheered.

I smiled and then let out a deep sigh of satisfaction. "I think it went really well. Whether I win or not, I'm psyched. It was the best presentation I could have done. I'm proud. Thank you all so much for your help. I could not have done it without you."

"What's up with the Lurker?" asked Emma, gesturing with her thumb behind her. Matt popped his head up from behind Emma and gave me a thumbs-up, and we all laughed.

"More like the Burper!" I said.

"Oh, boys are so gross," agreed Emma.

"Come see my table!" called Matt.

I looked at the other girls, unsure of what to do.

"You've got this," Mia said quietly.

"Go for it," said Emma.

"While you're riding high from your triumphant presentation," Katie said.

"Oh, what the heck, right?" I said cheerfully. "Please watch my booth, girls!" I ducked out from behind my table as they stepped into place to cover for me.

Matt looked surprised but definitely pleased I'd agreed, and he stuck out his elbow for me to hook my hand into so he could escort me down the aisle. I wanted to die, but I was also thrilled and terrified.

I was too nervous to look at any of the other exhibits as we passed, and I felt bad, since some of my friends were calling out to me. I just kept my eyes fixed on the horizon and enjoyed the sensation of floating with my hand on his warm arm.

All too soon, we were at Matt and Samantha's booth. It was kind of cheerful, and their model of the closed loop was big and impressive.

"Wow!" I said genuinely.

Samantha smiled. "Hi, Alexis. Do you like it?" she asked nervously.

I was pleased she knew my name. She could easily have forgotten it or pretended to not have known it.

"Hi, Samantha. It's really cool! How did you guys do this?" Once we were actually talking, I felt much calmer.

Samantha told me with excitement all about their theory and project, and I nodded along, even after she lost me halfway through her explanation. She also thanked me profusely for the cupcakes I had dropped off as a thank-you for her dad the week before. I'd been so nervous, my knees had knocked together at their door, but he had been really psyched and happy.

"Do you really like the model?" Matt asked after.

"Yes. It's great. You guys really know what you're doing, I can tell." Honestly, it was pretty dull to me, but I'm sure if you were a systems person, it was cool.

"Thanks!" Matt said happily. "Here, have a mint!" He offered me a bowl of wrapped candies.

"Thanks," I said, taking one and unwrapping it to pop into my mouth.

"Well, I should get back to my booth. I don't have a partner who can give my speech for me."

"It makes it a lot easier. Especially if you ask the best computer student in your class," agreed Samantha.

Matt smiled. "That's debatable."

My stomach clutched for a second, but when I stopped to think about it, I really didn't think I sensed anything between them.

"Good luck, you guys!" I said. "Thanks for the mint!"

"Thanks for the cupcakes!" replied Matt. "I'll come find you after!"

"Okay," I agreed. *Okay!*

You could have knocked me over with a feather when I won.

I mean this really and truly from the bottom of my heart: I did not think I was going to win. I knew I did my presentation well, and certainly, edible treats never hurt. But what the judges told my science teacher they liked was my attention to detail, and also that my topic was timely and related to kids.

The prize was five hundred dollars!

But the real prize was that Matt Taylor hugged me when I won.

And so did my friends.

That night, Emma called me after dinner. My mom had made steak to celebrate my win, which was kind of ironic as it is not exactly healthy, so she never serves it. But I do love it!

"Lex!" Emma said in an urgent whisper.

"What?" I whispered back urgently.

"I have some news for you."

"What?" I whispered. "Good or bad?"

"Good," whispered Emma.

"Do we have to keep whispering?"

"Well, you don't," Emma murmured.

"Okay, what is it?" I asked in a normal voice.

"At dinner tonight, my parents were talking about how great your project was and how psyched and proud they were that you won, and Matt said, 'I wish she had asked me to be her partner.' Can you believe it?"

"Really? Seriously?"

"Yup!" Emma wasn't whispering anymore.

"Well, maybe he just wanted to be on the winning team?" I said.

"Oh, Lex. He went into a whole thing about how Samantha is so aggressive and she asked him to be her lab partner, and he wanted to be with Tommy Humphries, but it was awkward because Tommy was across the room, so he had to say yes to Samantha. Then she pushed him into doing the project with him, and it wasn't that fun or interesting and get this"—her voice dropped to a whisper—"he said, 'Things are always fun with Alexis.'"

I sat at my desk, openmouthed in shock.

"Lex?"

"Did he really say that, or are you making it up?"

"Alexis Becker, if you call me a liar one more

time, I am hanging up! Seriously, you're being ridiculous!"

"Sorry, sorry, sorry. Wow. That's . . . that's so nice. I'm flattered."

"Yeah, well, then guess what I said?"

"What?"

"I said, 'I thought you were all into Samantha Perry. She's into you!' And he said, 'I didn't realize it until she asked me to Martine's sweet sixteen. And that's when I had to say no. I just didn't want to give her the wrong idea. I mean, she's a great science student and all, but a sweet sixteen is a date, and I'm not going there.'"

"This is such awesome news! I'm pinching myself right now!" I squealed.

"It gets even better! So, I said, 'She's really pretty though, right?'"

"Emma! You traitor!" I cried.

"No, I just wanted to be sure I left no stone unturned, you know. So, he said, 'Well, she's not my type.'"

"So, what's his type?" I begged.

Emma laughed. "Well, that's exactly what *I* said! And then Sam was teasing him and said, 'Sporty, redheaded, cute, likes to bake . . .' And we all laughed . . ."

"Thanks a lot! Now your whole family is mocking me! I'm hanging up!"

"Stop! Get this—Matt just smiled! Normally, he would have killed Sam!"

"Wait, really?"

"Yup! Happy early birthday! That's your present! You're Matt's type!"

"That is the best present ever! Thank you so much!"

"My pleasure. Glad to be of service," joked Emma.

"Wow. What a great day," I said happily.

"I know. Congrats, dude!" said Emma.

"Thanks. Thanks for being such a great pal. Even if you *are* a model!"

"Now, *I'm* the one hanging up!" teased Emma.

I sat there, beaming and hugging myself. What awesome news. I guess it is true what Katie said: There is always more than meets the eye. I need to stop jumping to conclusions and just relax and live my life, and things will work out! Realizing this was even better than the news about Matt or the award.

*There's always more than meets the eye.* I guess I have a new motto!

Want another sweet cupcake?

Here's a sneak peek

of the next book in the

CUPCAKE DIARIES

series:

# Katie
# just
# desserts

## S'More Surprises

"Steady, Mia," I told one of my best friends.

That's because Mia Vélaz-Cruz was using a blowtorch, which is unusual for Mia since she's more likely to be holding a makeup brush or a sketch pencil or a sewing needle. She's very creative and artistic. And that's what she was using the blowtorch for—to make art. Out of cake frosting.

The community college near our town, Maple Grove, had announced a baking contest a few weeks ago for kids ages ten to seventeen. You had to first send in a recipe for a cake, and if your recipe was chosen, you were invited to the college to bake your cake in their kitchens in the final contest round.

As soon as Mia and I heard about the contest,

we knew we wanted to enter. We're part of a cupcake baking business with our friends Alexis Becker and Emma Taylor called the Cupcake Club. Emma knew she had a modeling gig the day of the contest, and Alexis had a school business club fair she was helping to run, so Mia and I entered together.

Each baker was allowed one helper, and Mia and I agreed that I should bake and she should help. We're a good team that way. I am food obsessed, so I'm good at coming up with recipes. And Mia can make any food look mouthwateringly delicious.

So, the recipe I came up with was a s'mores cake—a chocolate cake with layers of fudge and crumbled graham crackers in between. But the best part of the cake was the marshmallow frosting, which would top the cake with soft, fluffy peaks and then browned with a blowtorch for that toasted marshmallow taste.

When Mia and I submitted the recipe, we hadn't thought too much about the blowtorch part. It looked easy when chefs used them on TV. But in real life, a blowtorch is kind of scary.

Luckily, monitors from the college were walking around the kitchens, making sure none of us kids were hurting ourselves with knives or stoves—or blowtorches. One of them walked over when he saw Mia holding the blowtorch.

"Do you know how to use that?" he asked.

"My stepdad, Eddie, showed me how," Mia replied. "He said it's the wimpiest blowtorch he could find, and I just have to twist it a tiny bit to let the flame come out. Like this."

Mia twisted the end, and a small flame burst from the torch.

The monitor nodded. "Good job," he said.

As he looked on, Mia carefully burned the tips of the marshmallow peaks so they turned a toasty brown color. Soon, our kitchen smelled just like a campfire!

"That's perfect, Mia!" I cried, clapping, and I saw the monitor smile.

An announcement came over the loudspeaker. "Five minutes until judging!"

I looked around our kitchen area. The college had a teaching kitchen for their cooking students. We each had a stainless-steel table as a work area, and an oven. Right now, our table was strewn with flour, powdered chocolate, and some spilled egg whites.

"I'll clean this up," I said. "Mia, just make the cake look as beautiful as possible!"

"You got it," Mia replied. "Katie, it already looks and smells awesome. I think we could win."

As I straightened up, I looked around the kitchen. Nine other contestants had made it to the finals. A few of the kids looked younger than Mia and I, who are in middle school. Most of the kids looked like they were in high school. And I had to admit, some of the cakes looked amazing. This one girl had a white layer cake with these beautiful flowers and butterflies made out of fondant, a paste made out of sugar, all over it.

"I don't know," I said. "Some of the cakes out there look amazing."

"Well, I think it all comes down to a matter of personal taste with these things, sometimes," Mia said. "Who are the judges, again?"

"There are five judges," I told her. "Two are professors here at the college, and then they got three food experts from the community. That's what the entry form said. I didn't read it too carefully."

I'm not exactly what you'd call a detail-oriented person. I knew that I had to make an amazing cake and that the prize was five hundred dollars. That's all I needed to know, right?

I noticed that I was nervously tapping my purple sneaker on the floor. I took a deep breath. This was it! We had baked our hearts out. I knew my cake was delicious. And thanks to Mia, it was beautiful. There was nothing left to do but wait to be judged.

I glanced at my station. The stainless steel gleamed brightly, and the cake looked perfect on a black pedestal cake stand. There wasn't a stray crumb or fleck of icing anywhere.

Mia looked around. "Do you think this is what it will be like when you go to cooking school?"

"I guess," I said. (Mia and I had a dream: After high school, we would both go to school in Manhattan. I would train to be a chef at one of the big cooking schools in New York, and Mia would go to one of the fashion schools there.) "This is a pretty nice kitchen. I don't know if the school in New York will be fancier than this."

"This is good practice, anyway," Mia said. "We should enter the contest every year."

Then we heard another announcement. "Let the judging begin!"

A bunch of judges wearing white chef's coats entered the kitchen. A woman with a blond ponytail approached our table first. She was smiling and looked nice, so I relaxed a little—just a little.

"Ooh! 'S'mores Cake,'" she said, reading aloud from the recipe card posted at our station. "What a clever idea. I was a Girl Scout, you know."

Mia nudged me, and we were both thinking the same thing. We had definitely won this judge over!

She carefully cut a thin slice of cake, put it on a plate, and took a bite.

"Very moist," she said. "The cookie crumble adds some nice texture. And the toasted marshmallow is wonderful."

"Thank you!" Mia and I said together, and I felt like I was beaming from head to toe.

The next judge was a short woman who wore her brown hair in a bun. She didn't smile at us. She read the recipe card and then tasted the cake. She nodded, put down the plate, and then started writing in a little pad. She didn't say a word to us!

"Oh boy," Mia said as the second judge walked away. "Does that mean she didn't like it?"

"I'm not sure," I whispered back. "Maybe that's just her judging style."

The next judge who walked up was a tall guy with dark hair. He looked vaguely familiar. And then I noticed his name tag: MARC DONALD BROWN.

That's when the whole world froze around me.

Marc Donald Brown is my dad.

My dad, who left me and my mom when I was really little.

My dad, who moved back to New Jersey recently with a whole new family.

My dad, who e-mailed me saying he wanted to meet me, but I turned him down. I wasn't ready.

And here he was, judging my cake.

Marc Donald Brown was smiling when he came to the table. Then he looked at me. I was wearing a name tag too: KATIE BROWN.

Marc Donald Brown got a weird look on his face. We both stared at each other.

Then my legs took on a life of their own. Some primal instinct took over and I ran. I ran as fast as I could out of that room, and I didn't look back.

# So Awkward!

I stood outside in the college courtyard, gasping for air. I fumbled for my cell phone in my apron pocket and dialed the number of my mom's dental practice.

"Oh, hey, Katie," Joanne, the receptionist, said cheerfully.

"Can I talk to her?" I asked.

"Sorry, your mom's in the middle of a tooth extraction," Joanne said. "Are you okay? You sound upset."

"No, no, I'm . . ." I couldn't quite bring myself to say I was fine. Because I definitely wasn't.

"I'll have her call you back as soon as she gets out, okay, hon?" Joanne asked.

"Yeah, sure," I said. I ended the call and sat down

on a bench. I needed to collect my thoughts.

Mia raced up to me.

"Oh my gosh, Katie! I wasn't sure why you ran out, and then I saw the name on the judge, and I figured it out," she said. She put her arm around me. "You must be freaking out."

"I am," I said. I looked at her. "Mia, I'm sorry. I can't go back in there. Forget the contest. Let's just go home, okay?" My eyes started to fill with tears as I talked.

Mia nodded. "Of course. I'll call my mom to pick us up. I left my cell phone inside. I'll be right back."

Mia ran back inside, and I took some deep breaths, trying to process.

When Marc Donald Brown had first e-mailed me, he said he wanted us to meet and talk. He wanted me to meet his family. I just couldn't do it. For one thing, I wasn't sure how I felt about a dad who took off and then waited more than an entire decade before trying to see me again. Yeah, he sent birthday cards and stuff, but that's about it.

And what did he do in that time? The guy who apparently couldn't handle having a wife and a baby went out and found a *new* wife and then had three more babies—all girls. I know because Mia and I had this crazy idea to visit my dad's restaurant in Stonebrook, Chez Donald. (It's named that because he's always gone by his middle name, Donald.) I guess I thought I could maybe spy on my dad or something first, to see what he was like.

But I didn't even stay that long. I saw a newspaper article on the wall. I still remember the title. "Family Man Brings French Cuisine to Stonebrook." There was a photo of Marc Donald Brown with his new wife and three little girls. No mention of me at all, but why would there be? I freaked out and ran out of the restaurant—just like I had done in the college kitchen.

"Katie?"

A man's voice interrupted my thoughts. Marc Donald Brown was standing there.

"Uh, hi," I said. My heart was pounding like crazy.

"Mind if I sit down?" he asked.

"No, sure," I said. I couldn't look him in the face. I just couldn't. I just looked down at my apron and kept fumbling with the strings.

"I'm sure this must be awkward for you," he said. "It's awkward for me."

*Majorly awkward!* I thought, but I didn't say anything.

"I didn't know you were going to be in this contest," he said. "Otherwise, I would have tried to reach out beforehand."

"I didn't know you were going to be a judge," I mumbled.

"I still want to get to know you, Katie," MDB said. "Not like this, though."

"Oh, but you're such a family man," I found myself saying, remembering the article. "Don't you need to spend time with your other daughters?"

"This is the kind of stuff we need to talk about," he said. "Just please consider it. We can meet somewhere, just the two of us. There's a lot I need to say to you."

Something in his voice made me look up. His green eyes looked kind of sad.

"I'll think about it," I said.

"Okay," MDB said. He stood up. "By the way, your cake was delicious."

*Does he really think that, or is he just saying that?* I wondered. Something inside me really hoped he was being sincere. For some weird reason, it was important that Marc Donald Brown knew I was a good baker. That I was good at something.

Mia walked toward me as he walked away, and she raised her eyebrows.

"You okay?" she asked.

"I guess," I said. "He still wants to meet with me. I'm not sure if I want to, though. It's so weird!"

"Yeah, I can't imagine," Mia said.

I knew she couldn't. Mia's parents were divorced, like mine, but her dad never left the picture. Mia goes and stays with him in Manhattan every other weekend, and she spends half the summer with him too. He's not some stranger, like Marc Donald Brown.

Mia and I didn't talk anymore. We were quiet until her mom came to pick us up. Mrs. Valdes smiled and said hi, but then she didn't say anything either, so I knew Mia had told her what happened.

"Katie, you know you're welcome to come to our house for dinner," Mia's mom said as we got closer to my house.

"Thanks, I'm okay," I said. When the car pulled up, I muttered a good-bye and quickly ran out, let myself into my house, and then headed straight up to my bedroom.

Then I threw myself on my bed and cried and cried, and I wasn't even really sure why.

Coco Simon always dreamed of opening a cupcake bakery but was afraid she would eat all of the profits. When she's not daydreaming about cupcakes, Coco edits children's books and has written close to one hundred books for children, tweens, and young adults, which is a lot less than the number of cupcakes she's eaten. Cupcake Diaries is the first time Coco has mixed her love of cupcakes with writing.

Want more

# Cupcake Diaries?

Visit **CupcakeDiariesBooks.com**
for the series trailer, excerpts, activities,
and everything you need for throwing
your own cupcake party!

# Still Hungry?

## There's always room for another Cupcake!

CUPCAKE DIARIES
13
Katie's new recipe

CUPCAKE DIARIES
14
Mia a matter of taste

CUPCAKE DIARIES
15
Emma sugar and spice and everything nice

CUPCAKE DIARIES
16
Alexis and the missing ingredient

CUPCAKE DIARIES
17
Katie sprinkles & surprises

CUPCAKE DIARIES
18
Mia fashion plates and cupcakes

CUPCAKE DIARIES
19
Emma: lights! camera! cupcakes!

CUPCAKE DIARIES
20
Alexis the icing on the cupcake
by coco simon

CUPCAKE DIARIES
21
Katie starting from scratch

CUPCAKE DIARIES
22
Mia's recipe for disaster

CUPCAKE DIARIES
23
Emma's not-so-sweet dilemma

CUPCAKE DIARIES
24
Alexis's cupcake cupid

CUPCAKE DIARIES
25
Katie sprinkled secrets

CUPCAKE DIARIES
26
Mia the way the cupcake crumbles

CUPCAKE DIARIES
27
Emma raining cats and dogs . . . and cupcakes!

CUPCAKE DIARIES
28
Alexis cupcake crush

CAKE DIARIES
29
Katie just desserts

ICING

If you liked

CUPCAKE DIARIES

be sure to check out these

other series from

Simon Spotlight

If you like reading about the adventures of Katie, Mia, Emma, and Alexis, you'll love Alex and Ava, stars of the It Takes Two series!

# sew zoey

Zoey's clothing design blog puts her on the A-list in the fashion world . . . but when it comes to school, will she be teased, or will she be a trendsetter? Find out in the Sew Zoey series:

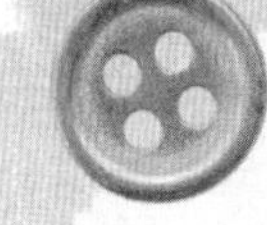

EVERY SECRET LEADS TO ANOTHER

# SECRETS of the MANOR

**Hidden passages, mysterious diaries, and centuries-old secrets abound in this spellbinding series. Join generations of girls from the same family tree as they uncover the secrets that lurk within their sumptuous family manor homes!**

EBOOK EDITIONS ALSO AVAILABLE

SecretsoftheManorBooks.com • Published by Simon Spotlight • Kids.SimonandSchuster.com

You're invited to MORE

# CREEPOVERS!

## HAVE YOU BEEN TO EVERY ONE?

Available at your favorite store!

CREEPOVERBOOKS.com